T0150198

Haunted Northern New York

– Volume 4 –

Cheri Farnsworth

North Country Books, Inc.
Utica, New York

ISBN-10 1-59531-035-5
ISBN-13 978-1-59531-035-4

Design by Zach Steffen & Rob Igoe, Jr.

Library of Congress Cataloging-in-Publication Data

Farnsworth, Cheri, 1963-
  Haunted northern New York IV / by Cheri Farnsworth.
      p. cm.
  Includes bibliographical references (p.   ).
  ISBN 978-1-59531-035-4 (alk. paper)
  1. Haunted places--New York (State) 2. Ghosts--New York (State) I.
Title. II. Title: Haunted northern New York 4.
  BF1472.U6F35 2010
  133.109747'5--dc22
                              2010036058

North Country Books, Inc.
220 Lafayette Street
Utica, New York 13502
www.northcountrybooks.com

Dedicated to my wonderful brother, Tom Dishaw.

Table of Contents

Bibliography

About the Author

Acknowledgments

First of all, my family deserves the most gratitude, of course, for bearing with me and letting me do my own thing, as time consuming as it often is. But I'm even more grateful for the fact that just seeing and being with them negates the effects my research would otherwise have on me. The stories I write are about real people, not fictional characters. I immerse myself daily into the intricate details of our ancestors' deaths—as brutal and horrifying as they sometimes were—attempting to understand why some of them have not "crossed over." It's the sobering nature of this work that reminds me of the frailty of life. So, to my husband, Leland Farnsworth, and my daughters, Nicole, Katie, Jamie, and Michelle Revai, thank you for keeping me in this moment and reminding me how precious and good life is. When I'm writing about dark and stormy nights, you brighten my days. I love you for that.

A big shout-out goes to the other VIPs in my life: my parents, Tom and Jean Dishaw; my brother, Tom—to whom I dedicate this book; and sisters Cindy Barry and Chris Walker (along with Ed, Rachel, Ryan, Danon, Heather, Amanda, Bryan, Cade, and Lindsey); and my in-laws, Carol and Lee Farnsworth. You guys are the best.

This book would not have been possible without the help of quite a few people who offered their personal experiences, recollections of others' experiences, suggestions for stories to research, and information they'd garnered from investigations or other sources. So, a big, hearty "thank you" goes to: Phil Creighton, Kate Heuser, and the Shadow Chasers, Timothy Abel, Merrill McKee, and the Northern New York Paranormal Research Society, Dean Frary and the Northern New York Paranormal Investigating Team, Dennis, Marc, and Sarah Spicer, Belle Salisbury, Leah Milot, Tom Scozzafava, Helen Condon, Margaret

Gibbs, Carmela Mayette, Aubrianna, Christopher, and Shannon Nye, Jan Couture, Stacey Tarbox, Betsy Baker, Gary Remington, Ron Streeter, Christina, and Bud. Thank you all for your time and patience.

Special thanks to the Northern New York Library Network for its herculean effort in putting together the greatest online resource ever for local history buffs like me. The *Northern New York Historical Newspapers* online archive consists of scanned images of nearly one and a half-million pages of old newspapers—a truly invaluable resource that I hope everyone will check out.

To Rob Igoe and Zach Steffen at North Country Books, what can I say? Here we are at book number four in this series! Thank you so much for your continued interest in the title, and for your expertise, friendship, and professionalism. I took my first baby steps in writing years ago, and I must say it's been a pleasure learning to walk with you.

Introduction

It was a dark and stormy night… How many times have those familiar words come to mind as I've sat at my laptop in my dimly-lit office, tapping feverishly on the keyboard while my family sleeps? For a decade I've been doing this on the side—writing about ghosts and researching the history of the places they inhabit into the wee hours of the morning. In August 2000 (ten books ago in "author-speak"), I wrote the first story for my first book, *Haunted Northern New York*. There were already works, both old and new, about Adirondack ghosts by other authors. But that book and its subsequent volumes were the only ones out there specific to ghosts in the rest of the vast North Country region—a fact I'm sure was not lost on my publishers when they chose to publish the series. (Writer's tip: Publishers love it when you have a good book idea in an untapped market, especially when the subject matter is enjoying a sudden rise in popularity.) And, man, was the paranormal hot. Ghost stories were sizzling. The timing couldn't have been better. Almost overnight, the relatively-hushed topic of ghosts had found its voice…and an eager audience. People have always been fascinated by ghost stories, especially in the late 1800s and early 1900s, when every community scrambled to locate a "spook" to call its own. (Heaven forbid a neighboring community should have something the next one over didn't!) When the Jefferson County town of Philadelphia, for example, listed its annual statistics in the *Watertown Herald* in 1889, the article said, "We have one thousand inhabitants; forty-six marriageable daughters, seven teen[age] widows…a state bank, two saw mills…one of the finest hotels in the county, a haunted house on the lower end of Main Street, [and] a young man that has seen the ghost…" (Did it just say "forty-six *marriageable* daughters"?!)

These days we have people coming out of the woodwork to share their personal stories of both frightening ghostly visitations and reassuring spirit encounters, thus ensuring that each community has not just one, but many, haunted houses. Hollywood certainly knows this and is partially responsible for society's eager embrace of the subject matter. From popular shows like *Ghost Hunters* and *Paranormal State*, we have gleaned our cues about how to handle this delicate topic. Thanks to Hollywood—and to my fellow ghost authors around the country doing exactly what I do but in a different place—we've come to the conclusion that it's okay to talk about ghosts. So let's talk.

In literature, hauntings and history complement each other rather nicely. History makes ghost stories easier to explain, and ghost stories make history easier to recall. As a writer, I've evolved along with this realization. At first I was content to tell a story with little or no historical background, and that seemed to work fine. But now I find myself obsessing over the need to include some history with each story, at least wherever possible. I search for good, solid reasons for each haunting, in a field that is anything but solid. And if there's one thing I've learned from all of this, it's that the reasons are many and varied. For example, the incident at Slaughter Hill near Watertown in 1828—when Henry Evans killed two men with an axe while protecting his family and home—may have created three potential ghosts: the killer, who felt he had been unjustly hanged (and in front of a cheering mass of thousands, no less), and his victims, who were certainly caught unawares when they forcibly entered his home that day, intending only to evict him from their property.

Then there were the unsolved murders of Mary Desmond, of Burke, in 1906 and of a young, female servant of a Parishville preacher in the late 1800s—two North Country women who disappeared long ago, presumably victims of foul play. Their bodies (and their murderers) were never found, and the circumstances surrounding their deaths still remain unsolved. Spirits such as theirs are known to linger until their killers have been brought to justice or their murders are solved. Deadly crimes of the past can produce unhappy ghosts that we must confront in the future.

Sackets Harbor and Fort Ticonderoga, like many former battle-grounds, are rife with residual energy that can be both seen and heard. This type of haunting has no consciousness, so it's not possible to interact with it. Residual hauntings are best described as glimpses of the past, frozen in time, like an old record album with a skip that replays the same thing over and over. There are several scenarios that may result in a residual haunting. One is when a living person does something so often (i.e. walking up the same staircase, ringing the same old bell) that over time, energy of that action "rubs off" on the environment, leaving a vague impression that we can sense long after the action has ceased. Another is when a death occurs so violently and unexpectedly that an impression of what the individual was doing just a millisecond before that event becomes seared into the environment, like the skid marks a car leaves on the road just before it crashes. While residual hauntings seem to occur as often as traditional hauntings (in which the spirit tries to get our attention), there are more reasons for a conscious spirit to haunt one's property than there are for a residual haunting to exist.

Besides murder, conscious haunting can result from an unhealthy attachment to a person, place, or thing, like the spirits of previous owners that haunt the Paddock Mansion in Watertown or the helpful ghost at the Evans Mills Rescue Squad building. These spirits have worn out their welcome but are obviously in no hurry to leave, unless they can be convinced to do so. The female apparition seen wandering around the Hopkinton-Fort Jackson Cemetery is a good example of another type— someone who is unaware of his or her own death and continues to haunt a place.

Tragedies like suicide, accidental death, or death by illness may also result in hauntings. Examples include Mabel Smith Douglass haunting Pulpit Rock in Lake Placid where she drowned, the infants believed to haunt the LeRay and Paddock Mansions after dying there of disease, and the spirit of a heartbroken wife who haunts the BrightSide on Raquette, still waiting for her husband to return from an ill-fated trek into a deadly blizzard. In other cases, there are those deceased who may simply wonder why someone is invading what they believe to still be their property. Like the male spirit at 59 North Main Street in Massena whose sentiments regarding his right to remain in his old kitchen were heard loud and clear on an EVP, these spirits tend to make their objections known in no uncertain terms.

Finally, there's the proverbial unfinished business, which could apply to many different stories in this book, depending on what each spirit considered its unfinished business to be: Seeing its killer prosecuted? Setting the table one last time? Awaiting the recovery of his or her body? Awaiting the return of a loved one? Almost all of us have unfinished business when we cross over, since people are rarely prepared for their moment of passing, but, thankfully, most people don't allow such reasoning to hinder their progression to the Other Side.

On the following pages, you will see examples of every type of ghost story—new stories that have never been told before, previously-publicized stories that have long been forgotten but are resurrected here for a new generation of readers, old stories with continuing paranormal activity, stories of places haunted by a single memorable incident as well as those of prolifically-haunted locations, and legends passed down from generation to generation. I hope such a diverse assortment gives my readers a greater respect for the history that gave rise to these ghost stories.

Note: Where you see an asterisk (*) in the text, the name of the individual has been changed per his or her request.

"Dr. Drury, Charles Morrison, N.A. Jones, and John Schweiner of the Great Bend visited Felts Mills, Sunday night, to find the ghost in the haunted house of George Matondo. They sat up all night watching, took cold, and came home sick. Dr. Drury has them under his care, and they will probably be saved."

March 16, 1881
The Democrat—Lowville, NY

Warning: Ghost hunting may be hazardous to your health (and good sense).

Proceed at your own risk.

Nye Manor

Fort Covington

Like an actor straight out of one of Verizon's *Dead Zone* commercials, an elderly gentleman walking past 54 Covington Street recently wagged his finger at owner Christopher Nye, who was shoveling snow in his driveway, and blurted out unashamedly, "Your house is haunted." Then, in case Christopher hadn't heard him the first time, the old guy said it again, only with more conviction and a halting emphasis on the last word. "Your house is *haunted*!" It wasn't news to the Nyes, who bought the historic, Georgian-style stone manor on the corner of Center and Covington in 2005 and have been busy restoring it ever since. They've also been busy answering the door ever since, as a steady stream of people stop by to share their "Nye Manor" ghostly experiences with the new owners. Some are local kids who were in the house while it was vacant, but most are people who knew previous residents. One such individual told Christopher that a former owner, who lived there until she died of natural causes in 1968, used to talk about how she would occasionally find the table set with finery when she arose in the morning, even when she lived there alone. It seemed an obvious attempt to announce that she had company—albeit of the unseen kind.

The stone house was built in 1837 by Jabez Parkhurst, a prominent early lawyer, judge, and abolitionist. Old news accounts reported that his wife, Fidelia Man, was suffering from symptoms of "mental derangement" when she committed suicide in the front upstairs bedroom in 1849. It was said that she had been confined to the room, where she used needles and yarn to knit her own noose and hang herself from a high bed post. What could possibly have pushed someone to that ultimate act, deranged or not? Was it the loss of three beloved children in that same home, all before their first birthdays? Or was it the empty-nest syndrome she experienced following her daughter Caroline Parkhurst Gillette's marriage in 1848, just a year and a half before Fidelia's tragic departure? Tragically, Caroline hanged herself, just like her mother had, and left a suicide note with instructions to bury her next to her baby and mother in the Protestant Community (Old Fort Covington) Cemetery. According to Charles Gillette's obituary in *The Sun* on January 5, 1888, Caroline named her first (and only) child after her late mother.

> One daughter, Fidelia, was born of this union; she died in infancy. Overcome with grief over the irreparable loss, the distracted mother soon followed her infant daughter and was buried in the same grave at her request, August 1857.

Was it Caroline's or Fidelia's voice that Christopher heard in the bathroom one day when he was by himself in the house or on the night he puttered around the house alone and heard a female voice in the bathroom behind him say "hello?" It sounded like someone talking "through an echo chamber," he said, which I thought was a very clever way of explaining trans-dimensional acoustics. Shannon Nye also has heard unexplainable voices, as well as footsteps and doors closing when she has been the only one home. But what bothers her more are the feelings she occasionally gets when she walks through the front door. She might be in a terrific mood as she enters the house, only to be over-come almost immediately by inexplicable feelings of sadness and despair. Knowing what we do about the Parkhurst family's tragic past, we can assume Shannon is sensitive to (and therefore tapping into) the emotions experienced long ago by the earlier ladies of the house.

At some point prior to the start of the Civil War, the house had become a station on the Underground Railroad. After all, Jabez was the vice president of the abolitionist movement in New York State, and his stately home did have the requisite trap doors, underground tunnels, and close proximity to Canada—a mere half mile away. In fact, when the current owners first began renovations, Christopher searched in vain for

The Nye family.

the entrance to the basement that was used during the Underground Railroad period. He finally gave up and went for a power saw so he could cut a hole in the floor. But according to the October 2008 Post-Investigative Report prepared by Merrill McKee, founder of the Northern New York Paranormal Research Society (NNYPRS), when Christopher returned with the saw, a hatch that he hadn't noticed before was not only open, it was shamelessly propped up with a stick!

Mr. Parkhurst died of natural causes on Halloween Day, 1865, in the house where his first wife and children had tragically perished. In the late 1890s, the Dennis Denneen family took ownership. Theirs were happy years spent in Fort Covington: the yin of the Parkhurst family's yang. Margaret Denneen's obituary in *The Sun* from July 14, 1921, said the 82-year-old woman was "a model old-time mother. Not only was she [the] mother of a large and gifted family, but in a much larger sense, she was a mother to all with whom she came in contact." She and Dennis raised eight children there, and when Margaret Denneen died at a ripe old age, seven of their brood were still alive and well. In 1935, their daughter Genevieve returned from New York City following the death of her husband, Ralph Hayes, and moved into her childhood home, where she remained for more than thirty years. It was during that time that the first reported ghost stories surfaced.

In 1993, the vacant house suffered the effects of a suspicious fire and was purchased by the St. Regis Mohawk Tribe. When the Nyes bought it from the Tribe in 2005, they saved it from scheduled demolition. Before deciding for certain that he wanted to buy the old house, Christopher and his uncle went through it carefully. As they were walking through the darkened building, each carrying a brand new flashlight, they received their first glimpse of what was to come when they entered the library and both flashlights died. (Ghosts are known to drain batteries and wreak havoc on various sources of energy.) But the incident didn't change Christopher's mind about the place. Before ever reaching the library, he had already decided to buy the property, haunted or not.

The NNYPRS had their share of experiences to throw into the mix. At the start of their first investigation, the organization's vice president, Dave, was going upstairs when a sheetrock sanding pole tumbled from the landing above, almost hitting him. Christopher insists that the pole had not been in the stairwell that evening; in fact, he recalled seeing it elsewhere in the house. After the investigators left that night, the elusive pole thrower would give it another shot, this time directed at Shannon. She was going up the same stairs when the pole almost struck her—and this was after Christopher made absolutely certain to place it far away from the stairs after the earlier near-miss. The team attempted to recreate the pole-falling incidents, but they were unable to do so.

A feisty spirit also tried its hand at sheetrock tossing that night. Two of the team members, Randy and Brian, had just walked through an unexplainably cold area when a piece of sheetrock seemed to fly at them with some force, though there was nobody standing there who could have bumped into or pushed it. So they asked the entity to repeat that action, and another piece of sheetrock immediately fell to the floor, though with not nearly as much force as the first time. Merrill had the team attempt to recreate that incident and found that pieces of sheetrock could, in fact, fall if the floor in that room was jarred. However, Randy and Brian believe that the first piece of sheetrock came at them with more force than if it was simply falling naturally.

Several interesting sounds were recorded that night. Team members Nick, Dave, and Todd were all in the attic at around eleven thirty doing an electronic voice phenomenon (EVP) session when they heard (with their own ears) the muffled sound of a conversation that included a female voice. On tape, this was heard just after the sound of the front door opening and someone walking into the house, even though the rest of the group was taking a break at the time in the carriage house (garage), which was about a hundred feet away. Explaining what his crew experienced that night, Merrill told me:

> At first, they figured it had to be us outside the house talking. Using our radios, they contacted us, and we were still in the garage. The radio crackled, and they couldn't understand, so they focused on the sound. Once again, footsteps were heard, along with some other muffled talk. Approximately four minutes in [to the recording session], Christopher came into the house through the back door, up the back stairs, and could easily be heard. Another minute after that, the rest of the investigators left the carriage house to go to the main house. We have a very clear timeline, and it is impossible for any of our investigators or the family to be the sounds on the EVP.

Based on the evidence collected, as well as their own personal experiences, the NNYPRS decided after that initial visit that there was "sufficient data to tentatively conclude that this home is haunted."

Satterlee Hall

Potsdam

SUNY Potsdam's Satterlee Hall.

In the early 1950s, buildings started springing up on the present site of the State University of New York's (SUNY's) Potsdam campus after the State Teachers College at Potsdam joined the newly-formed State University system. Satterlee Hall, one of the first buildings on campus, opened in 1954 as the Benjamin Raymond Hall; with its landmark clock tower, it is easily identifiable as you drive past the college on Route 56/Pierrepont Avenue. Its name was changed in 1973, in honor of the college's former Director of Education and First Dean of Education, O. Ward Satterlee, who died of a heart attack while sitting at his desk in the building on April 3, 1970.

When the building first opened, the impressive College Theater it housed offered state-of-the-art equipment and seated up to eight hundred people. Today, both the original theater (the main stage used for traditional drama productions) and the smaller Black Box Theater (for non-traditional programs) are located in Satterlee, along with offices for the Department of Theatre and Dance staff. There are also reports of some less-tangible occupants of the building that give new meaning to the theatrical term "stage fright." Enter Shadow Chasers.

Phillip Creighton and Kate Heuser are cofounders of the Shadow Chasers, a team of local paranormal investigators. Both SUNY Potsdam graduates, their collective knowledge on the subject is as impressive as the vast array of high-tech equipment they take with them on investigations. The Shadow Chasers were brought in to investigate unusual happenings in the costume closet. Phil reported:

> After placing the recorder in the Costume Closet, we moved to the end of the hall, blocking access, and waited on it. When we went to retrieve it, I set foot in the room and walked right into the high energy field/ghost. As I backed out of the room with the recorder, one of our members said, "You look like you fell out of the room, like you were hit." I told the others to set their foot in there and pointed to the doorway. They tried walking through the door, resulting in a *Whoa!* and them staggering out of the room. I started playing the recorder back in front of the team, along with the small group of drama people that got us access. Halfway through the track, we heard a dog bark and immediately I was stunned. I was expecting voices, murmuring, or something of that nature—not a dog! I played it three more times, and everyone was in agreement that it was a dog. While we

listened, I took note that everyone had gradually drifted away from the open door, apparently sensing something in the doorway.

While the voice on the recordings didn't sound like the spirit of the old woman rumored to haunt that room, it did sound like a rat terrier or some other type of little dog that was clearly growling or yelping—and there was definitely no such critter in the room, or anywhere in the vicinity, for that matter. A month later, when the team checked out the costume room again, the same sound was heard, not once, but five times in one recording. I was amazed at the clarity of the EVP when I heard it. It seems to validate the story one student had previously admitted to the Shadow Chasers about having to leave that room while attempting to retrieve something off a shelf because she was alarmed by the barking of an invisible little dog.

I found no record of the demise of a dog in Satterlee Hall—but also nothing to indicate that there *hadn't* been such a death. Or maybe a past performer occasionally left his or her dog sequestered in that room (a makeshift kennel) during performances. If so, perhaps the protective pet became accustomed to guarding the closet room in life and continues to guard its familiar digs even today.

Spicer Home

Malone

The Spicer home.

Marc and Sarah Spicer had looked at dozens of homes in Malone before they found the one that really spoke to them (and I do mean, *really* spoke to them) in 2002. As soon as they walked through the door of the 180-year-old house at 19 Wellington Street, they said it felt like home. They knew they belonged there. A week after moving in, they were married on their back deck (where shadowy figures would later be spotted), and everything was going along just swimmingly, until…

Early one morning in the spring of 2003 while Sarah was visiting her parents, Marc was awakened when he heard someone sneezing downstairs. It sounded like a man. *Was it an intruder?* Whomever it was, he was definitely in the room below the bedroom, so Marc called the police and asked the officer to stay on the line as he searched the house, cordless phone in hand. After a thorough search, Marc conceded that nobody had broken in, and he apologized to the policeman.

The following year was a year of changes. Marc and Sarah were remodeling their home when their baby daughter was born, so not only was the house changing, but its residents were as well. And we all know that ghosts aren't big fans of change, so it shouldn't be surprising that the couple began experiencing unexplained phenomena the next year. They saw shadows moving in the corner of their reading room upstairs, the same corner their two cats seemed to love, for some reason they couldn't fathom. But since pets are inherently drawn to children, they began to wonder if there was perhaps a child's spirit haunting their home, a possibility that became almost a certainty when they began to hear the sound of a small child running overhead when they and their cats were downstairs. When their daughter was not yet two and just beginning to put words together, she started pointing to nothing they could see, saying "pretty baby" or "nice baby." She would reach her hand out as if stroking someone's face and yell out, "Hello, Baby!" These interactions always seemed to occur right near her bedroom door, close to the second floor stairway landing. In that same location, guests have admitted seeing a "shadowy figure" floating up the stairs.

One night Marc was awakened by the sound of someone yelling, "Jane!" Just as he began to fall back asleep, he heard the same shout again. It was a woman's voice, and she meant business. It was the middle of the night, and he could tell that the voice was coming from within his house, as the windows were all closed. The voice was clear, loud, and distinctive. He said it sounded like a concerned mother calling to a child. Marc got up, checked out every nook and cranny of his home, and came up empty-handed, just as he had two years earlier. While the incident was still fresh on his mind the following morning, his daughter suddenly blurted out, "Jane! Jane!" repeating the words with the same urgency that Marc had heard in the woman's voice during the night. She had either heard and was mimicking the same woman, or this Jane person was the "pretty baby" the little girl kept talking to outside her bedroom door. If the latter was the case, the spectral woman who called to Jane may have been her mother or some other female relative or maybe a nanny. It was becoming apparent that there were both male and female (and young and old) presences in the Spicer home.

On several occasions, Marc and Sarah heard hammering and whistling in their house; each time, they ruled out the possibility that the sound was coming from outside. Marc has heard his name whispered in the middle of the night, and for a stint of several consecutive nights, he awakened at exactly 2:52 A.M. During a different time period, their daughter woke up screaming at precisely midnight for several nights in a row. There seemed to be a pattern or a message that someone was intent on delivering to the family, but what it was remains to be seen.

Sarah's paranormal experiences occurred mostly in the upstairs bathroom, where she and Marc actually witnessed two doors opening and closing right before their eyes, even though the doors are evenly hung and would require physical manipulation to push or pull them open. Sarah heard names being called and whistling while in the bathroom, and Marc heard hammering there. The room also caused Sarah to feel dizzy, especially while in the shower, and I felt the same sensation while just walking through the room. Marc told me that at one point, "a strange smell emanated from under the easternmost sink" in the bathroom. Several contractors and plumbers were unable to determine the source of the smell, but after local psychic Belle Salisbury visited the Spicers in 2006, the smell disappeared.

Belle owned the Whispering Willow on Main Street in Massena and was often consulted for her expertise with haunted homes. I wrote about her work extensively in *Still More Haunted Northern New York*. Much of what the Spicers suspected about their home being haunted by several spirits was confirmed by Belle. Though she was given no specific information regarding the paranormal activity or the home's history, she was quickly drawn to the hotspots in the house, where she sensed exactly what the Spicers had been experiencing. The first place Belle headed was the bathroom, which the Spicers agree was the most active room in the house, in a paranormal sense. She pointed into the room, then looked at the couple and asked if either had ever experienced dizziness in there, which, of course, Sarah had. Belle said the heightened spirit activity in that room was a drain on the energy of the living (spirits need energy to manifest), and the energy drain was what caused the dizziness. Next, Belle headed toward the Spicers' daughter's room. Standing just outside the door where their daughter communicated with someone they couldn't see, Belle felt the spirit of a baby girl about eighteen months old. She also sensed an older woman—a nanny—in the back corner of their daughter's bedroom, where Belle said the nanny once rocked the child. Was the nanny the voice that Marc had heard, and was Jane the baby girl she had called to? It seemed a distinct possibility after getting Belle's inside scoop. The child, Belle said, had not been healthy, and her illness was the cause of her death. Marc provided the photograph below that appears to show a toddler's face on the metal ash can in their driveway in front of the garage. Furthermore, childlike writing in chalk was discovered on a wall in the garage when Marc removed an old peg board. As he tried to wipe the chalk away, the ladder behind him began to teeter, as if someone were standing on it precariously, looking over his shoulder to see what he was up to.

Photo provided by Marc Spicer.

Image of toddler face on ash can.

Besides the spirit energy in the bathroom, the toddler, and the nanny, Belle also sensed a presence in the reading room, where the Spicers used to see shadows moving, and on the back deck, where the couple was married. She felt the presence of a very tall and frail "handyman type," which might explain the sounds of hammering, whistling, and sneezing that had been heard. I just wonder if he was handy enough to concoct the putrid smell that had been emanating from under the bathroom sink. After Belle's visit, the smell never occurred again. By acknowledging the presence of spirits in the bathroom, had she unwittingly set some of them free? It seems that often all they want is to be noticed and acknowledged one more time before crossing over.

Also in 2006, the Shadow Chasers investigated the home and left with an abundance of evidence of paranormal activity that includes remarkable photographs depicting various forms of spirit energy—orbs, vortices (a chain of orbs all headed in one direction), and ectoplasm, including a long streak in the location where Belle said the nanny rocked the little girl. They also got a lot of video footage "from a remote camera of hundreds of orbs all travelling in different directions," according to cofounder Kate Heuser.

In the fall of 2007, Marc told me that things "went kinda nuts" at their house, paranormally speaking, when both he and Sarah started seeing a little girl's spirit—presumably the same child ghost that their daughter often seemed to interact with.

> I awoke in the middle of the night, probably around 2 A.M., and wondered why our three-year-old was sitting on the edge of the bed on Sarah's side. I braced myself up on my elbow and realized that the little girl in the bed was not our daughter. The little girl caressed Sarah's cheeks and held her hand to her own chest. Then I realized I could see right through her! I tried to wake up Sarah, but when I did, the child's image turned as clear as glass. Then she faded from head to foot.

Sarah saw a similar apparition a few weeks later. She described it as a little girl of about three years of age wearing an old-fashioned white dress. When Sarah saw her standing in the doorway between the kitchen and the middle room, she stopped and said hello. With that, the apparition faded before her eyes, as if dissolving from top to bottom. The couple then called in another local psychic, who told them she believed a seven-year-old girl had been killed accidentally in the house more than a hundred years earlier and was buried in the basement. The apparition the Spicers had seen was definitely younger, but they always knew they had more than one spirit sharing their home with them. During an EVP session in the kitchen, that same psychic called for the original owner of the house to indicate his or her presence with a knock or a word. She asked if the spirit wanted the Spicers to leave, at which point a distinct knock was later heard on playback. Also in the kitchen, shoes and other small objects came up missing, only to reappear days later in an obvious spot that could not have been overlooked, like in the middle of the countertop.

Photo by Shadow Chasers.

Energy vortex (orbs in motion).

After the Spicers first began seeing the full-blown apparition of the little girl, they called in the Malone-based Northern New York Paranormal Research Society. With founder Merrill McKee at the helm, the group dispersed throughout the house, armed with various types of paranormal gear. Marc participated in the investigation and said:

> When we were in the reading room upstairs, I called for the little girl. I felt the strangest sensation…as if a child were snuggling in my lap. I also had the inexplicable feeling that there was a frightened child nearby. Merrill used a laser thermometer and discovered that the area of my chest and stomach where it felt like the child was snuggling had dropped ten degrees lower than that of my shoulder! This was videotaped. Several people who were present took pictures with flashes. At one point, there was an unidentified shadow on a wall opposite me that was not repeated during any of the other flashes that night.

A few weeks after the NNYPRS investigation, the Spicer's daughter went into their bedroom one night complaining of "a green old lady in her room who was telling her to be quiet and go to sleep." Marc immediately called a pastor friend who advised him that he had to get rid of the ghosts. He was told to go into each room of the house and anoint it with olive oil while saying a specific prayer. Marc immediately did as he was told, but he didn't tell Sarah or his daughter what he was up to. After the mission was accomplished, he returned upstairs, only to hear his young daughter say, "You're making the ghosts sad, Daddy." Sad or not, whatever he did that night seems to have worked. The Spicer residence has been paranormally inactive for about a year now.

Mayette Home

Massena

Mayette residence, Halloween 2008. Notice all of the orbs.

In the late 1800s, some of the homes being built on farmland along North Main Street in Massena served at times as single-family dwellings and at other times as boarding houses. Like any transient property from which many people come and go, the latter seem to have a higher-than-average chance of becoming haunted. And when a nearby cemetery is just a stone's throw from your back yard, the possibility of encountering spectral visitors in such a location will increase exponentially. The house at 59 North Main Street is a prime example. There is no doubt someone is haunting it, but specifically who it is, we've yet to determine.

Carmela Mayette has been living at the address on and off for over twenty years. Her parents bought the house in the 1980s, when she was just a toddler, and today she and her mother are co-owners. In 2008 Carmela was living there with her former fiancé, Jordan, and fifteen-month-old Aubrianna. Their daughter had been babbling to someone they couldn't see for some time, pointing to the top of the stairs, for example, and waving while saying "hi." In the basement, she sometimes would point to an empty corner near the furnace and talk to someone unseen. Another youngster who has visited the family several times somberly reported one day that there were "more people in the house than just us," admitting that it troubled him. They didn't realize what he meant at first. But they certainly do now. Children seem to have a much stronger sense about these things than most adults, as Aubrianna and the other child demonstrated—and a local psychic later confirmed what the kids have been sensing.

One night, just as the couple was going to bed, they heard a faint conversation downstairs, so Carmela asked Jordan to go down to check it out and see if maybe she had left the TV on. She hadn't. No source for the conversation was ever found. Then, one day when Jordan was home alone, he was in the basement puttering around when he heard the sound of heavy footsteps on the hardwood floor overhead. If that wasn't strange enough, the basement door suddenly swung closed. This incident, coupled with Aubrianna's unexplainable behavior and the mysterious conversations they had heard that night, prompted the two to call in Carmella's friend and coworker Dean Frary and his Northern New York Paranormal Investigating Team (NNYPIT). The PIT's local clairvoyant, Dennis, who visited the house with a team of investigators, saw several spirits: an older male in the attic that watches over the house, a tall man dressed in a suit standing in the corner where a female spirit was laid out to be viewed, and a little girl who looked about four years old. He also said that at one time long ago, there had been "heavy traffic" in the house, with many people coming and going on a regular basis. Today the house is a one-family residence, but when it was a boarding house a hundred-some years ago, many people did pass through its doors.

After being told that Dennis had seen the spirit of a woman laid out to be viewed and of a tall man dressed in a suit who stood nearby (her husband, perhaps?), I began researching newspaper archives regarding the address to see if there was anything to explain such a vision. There was. In 1973, a woman passed away at the age of 69, and according to her obituary, her body was placed "in repose" in the house at 59 North Main—another reason for the heavy traffic the clairvoyant reported. Prior to the NNYPIT's visit to the home, team members were unaware of this woman's passing or the fact that her body had been laid out in the home. In fact, they all stressed to me that the psychic had not been told anything regarding the experiences of the family currently living there now or of the home's history. Carmela told me that during the investigation, when the investigators were in the kitchen acquiring EVPs, Dennis told her that there had been a couple of wakes in the kitchen and that she should not be surprised if she sometimes picked up on the intense emotions of the past, such as grief and anger. Just as he was explaining this to her, an EVP captured a man's voice in the kitchen saying yes, as if in complete agreement, and it definitely wasn't the voice of anyone in the room.

Dennis also told the couple that the young female spirit plays with Aubrianna in the daytime and plays with her toys in the middle of the night. Dennis sensed that her death had something to do with stairs. She made her presence known at least twice during the investigation. First, Carmela felt someone poke her in the back (like when someone sneaks up on you and tries to startle you with a sharp jab) at the top of the stairs next to Aubrianna's room. Nobody was behind her, but they would later find out while playing back the audio that at precisely the same moment Carmela felt the poke, a little girl is heard giggling. It did not sound at all like Aubrianna, who was sleeping in a playpen on the first floor while the investigators were upstairs. Dennis was saying that he could feel the energy of the little girl spirit strongly beside them when Aubrianna woke up crying downstairs. He immediately felt the spirit's energy depart and, on a hunch, went down to see if he could sense her presence near Aubrianna's playpen. As suspected, the child spirit had run to her crying little buddy when she heard the toddler wake up.

Two nights after the investigation, Carmela began hearing footsteps in the attic and unexplained noises coming from the kitchen. One night while she lay in bed, she heard a cupboard door in the kitchen shut and thought that perhaps it was her cat (since it knows how to open cupboard doors), but just as she entertained that idea, the cat crawled out from under the bed. It hadn't been downstairs after all.

In my research, I found references to this particular street address in newspaper articles dating back as far as 1872, when a newlywed couple named Cline lived there. By the 1890s it had become a boarding house, first under P.F. Kezar and later run by James Lahey. A local restaurateur named William O'Neill bought it in 1907, along with the adjacent house, and lived in one or the other for nearly twenty years. Towards the end of Mr. O'Neill's life, he rented out the property in question while living in the house next door (where both he and his wife died, he in 1926 and she in 1940).

From 1926 through the mid-1980s, many different tenants passed through the doors of 59 North Main—just as Dennis had sensed—but I found no evidence of any violent deaths or tragedies that occurred on the premises. It's like any old house where many people had lived—there have been moments of great joy, when children were born to the occupants and newlyweds returned there from their honeymoons, and there have been times of sadness, when owners passed away or tenants lost their loved ones. So who is haunting this home, and why? The adult spirits may be previous owners, but the little girl ghost is an enigma. Dennis said she indicated that the house had changed and that some interior walls had been moved farther out to make the rooms bigger. This would suggest that she may have lived (and possibly died) in the house and is connected to it in that way or that she chose to haunt the house for an entirely different reason and has been doing it for many years. Maybe it has to do with the fact that the only thing separating the house from Pine Grove #2 cemetery (which we'll get to later in this book) is the two hundred feet of lawn and trees in the back yard. And what do restless spirits do? They wander. It's not like somebody is standing there in the graveyard telling them they can't hop over its property lines. In either scenario, we can only hope that someone (from our dimension or the spirit world) rescues this poor child's soul and shows her the way "home." There's nothing that gets to me more than stories involving young, helpless spirits.

Moriah Town Hall

Port Henry

The village of Port Henry lies in the town of Moriah on the shore of Lake Champlain. It's famous for its Champ (the Lake Champlain monster) sightings, as documented in my 2005 book, *Haunted New York: Ghosts and Strange Phenomena of the Empire State*. But lake monsters aren't the only "strange phenomena" known to the locals. The Moriah Town Hall at 38 Park Place in Port Henry has long been rumored to be haunted, and if anyone can vouch for those stories, it would be the Moriah Town Supervisor, Tom Scozzafava. He admittedly has "been around the town hall most of [his] life," not only as town supervisor for nearly twenty years, but also as Superintendent of Buildings & Grounds, a position he held prior to his extended stint as supervisor. As a result, he is intimately familiar with every nook and cranny of the historic property, as well as the history and ghost stories connected to it.

Tom recently told me that he and others have experienced "strange events" at the town hall over the years. He admitted that while working alone in the building at night, there have been times when he has heard doors close on the second floor of the three-story building, "mumbled voices" that sounded as if they were coming from the basement, and the sound of someone walking around on the third floor, where passersby swear they've seen an apparition of a man looking out the window. For no particular reason, local residents have dubbed the third-floor spirit "Fred." But Scozzafava suggests that perhaps it's the spirit of Fred Ring, an attorney for the Witherbee, Sherman Company, one of several large mining companies that operated iron mines in Moriah in its mining heyday. From the time they built it in 1875 until it was auctioned off in a foreclosure sale in 1933, the company used the elaborate French Second Empire building as their lavish administrative headquarters.

Though many people believe the spirit that haunts the town hall is someone who died *inside* the building while it was under W.S. & Co. ownership, I was unable to locate any documentation supporting that theory. However, I *did* find one news article from the *Plattsburgh Sentinel* dated August 17, 1883, about a woman who burned to death right in front of the building:

> Johanna Kennedy of Clayburgh, Clinton County, aged twenty-two years, a domestic living at James H. Allen's in Port Henry, was fatally burned last Sunday morning at about 7 o'clock…She attempted to light the fire in the cook stove with kerosene oil, when her clothing caught fire. Charles Van Etten, the night telegraph operator at the depot, heard her screams and was the first to see her as she was coming out of the house all ablaze. He ran to her and caught her just in front of Witherbee, Sherman & Co.'s office and pulled the burning clothing from her. In doing so, his clothing caught fire and he had to throw his coat off to save himself.

So a young woman once burned to death right in front of the Moriah Town Hall. Does her soul seek refuge in the last building she ever laid eyes on? There's no law that says you must die inside of a building in order to haunt it. Ghosts can haunt a place for a plethora of reasons, but generally it seems that the individual had some sort of connection to the structure, whether they worked there, built it, lived in it, fell in or out of love or had some other sort of life-altering experience there, or perhaps had a bone to pick with someone who owned the property. There were a number of individuals who suffered horrible, tragic deaths while working in the mining operations of Witherbee, Sherman, even if not inside their Park Place headquarters. Nineteen-year-old Walter Kennedy of Mineville was killed instantly in 1930 when "his clothes became caught in a revolving shaft at Mill No. 4, Witherbee, Sherman Co." He was "hurled around" violently and thrown to the floor and was already dead by the time coworkers reached him. And poor John Sweeney. He was employed as a "powder monkey" at Witherbee, Sherman at the time of his accidental death in 1889. He became extremely intoxicated after work one evening, staggered alone down a Port Henry road, and stopped to rest outside of Butterfield's barber shop at around midnight. He must have attempted to lean back on the railing above the basement but instead tumbled backwards over the side, striking his head on the concrete ten feet below. He didn't die immediately. In fact, the doctor thought he might survive, although in a partially paralyzed state. However, just after being placed in a wagon that was to transport him home, he passed away.

Each of the aforementioned individuals had some kind of tie to the old Witherbee, Sherman building that is now the Town Hall. Any one of them may have come back to haunt the premises. Or perhaps it's someone different altogether—like Fred, the company lawyer, as Scozzafava suggested. Were it not for that pesky publisher's deadline, I could spend days researching old newspaper articles, and I'm sure I'd dig up any number of additional accidents involving people somehow associated with the building or its former owners.

Hopkinton-Ft. Jackson Cemetery

Hopkinton

If you live near a cemetery long enough, there's a pretty good chance you'll catch a glimpse of something you'll never be able to explain. Local cemeteries are rife with spirit energy and paranormal activity, so I've written about them often. But one I somehow missed in previous works is the old Hopkinton-Ft. Jackson Cemetery on County Route 49 in Hopkinton—home of the little old lady in a long blue dress.

This cemetery is a favorite for paranormal investigators. The Shadow Chasers of Potsdam and the Northern New York Paranormal Investigation Team have both provided information regarding the Hopkinton-Ft. Jackson Cemetery for this story. When the Shadow Chasers investigated the graveyard several years ago at dusk, they witnessed an oddly-shaped mist drift across the road, as if possessed by consciousness, and then—after seemingly checking them out—it casually drifted back again. Perhaps it was the spirit they later heard laughing with them (or *at* them—we'll never know which). When several members of the team were lightheartedly teasing each other during their investigation of the grounds, they discovered that they weren't the only ones laughing. One of the members was holding a unit called an Electrosmog Detector (ESD), which looks like a Star Trek beaming device. The object indicates when "electro-pollution" is present, allowing the user to hear what the energy fields sound like and audibly track the direction of static. The Detector emitted a sound described by Phil Creighton as "pulsating laughter," as if a ghost was amongst them, enjoying their graveyard humor.

The Shadow Chasers also took a photograph of what can best be described as a phantom tombstone, strange as that may sound. In the photograph, a long stick reaches horizontally behind several tombstones (see below), but when it gets to the stone on the far right, the tombstone appears to be semi-transparent, so you can see the stick right *through* it. After the film was developed and the freakish anomaly was discovered, the Shadow Chasers returned to the cemetery, only to discover that there was no such tombstone.

Photo by Shadow Chasers.

Phantom tombstone (to the far right) does not actually exist.

The first time I heard about the old woman in the blue dress who was apparently haunting the cemetery was from Dean Frary of the NNYPIT. He told me that a man who lives near the S-curve on County Route 49 across from the Hopkinton-Ft. Jackson Cemetery has seen the ghost and so has an employee of the Hopkinton Highway Department. I contacted Ron Streeter, the Highway Superintendent, and asked him if he was familiar with this story. He sure was, and he put me in touch with one of his men, Gary Remington, for details. The first thing Gary said to me when I asked him if it was true that he'd seen a woman at the cemetery was, "Oh, you mean my girlfriend?" Obviously, he's been teased enough about it that he tries to make light of the sighting. But he said he knows what he saw, and it wasn't his imagination. He was never a "real big believer" in ghosts, he said, until a few years ago when the incident occurred.

It was a late fall day, and Gary was driving past the cemetery with a truckload of sand (in preparation for the approaching winter season) when he noticed a woman walking through the graveyard. Because it was cold out and she was dressed so inappropriately for the weather, he slowed down to get a better look. He described her as a little old lady wearing a ground-length, blue dress with very puffy short sleeves that had white trim around them. It was something you don't see people wear anymore…a hundred years ago, maybe, but not today. Her white hair was pulled up high in a bun on top of her head, and she was wearing little round spectacles. As he watched her walk past a bunch of maples, Gary remembered thinking how cold she must be with those short sleeves. And then, right before his eyes, she vanished from a spot in front of a tombstone in the middle of the cemetery. Unfortunately, from his vantage point, it was impossible to determine precisely which gravesite she was standing at because the cemetery is so large and densely populated with tombstones.

In a store some time later, Gary saw the gentleman mentioned above who lives right near where the sighting occurred. He had heard about Gary's encounter (news travels fast in small towns) and said something like, "So, I hear you met my friend." Gary was stunned when the man proceeded to describe his "friend" exactly as Gary had described his "girlfriend" to me. They had to be one and the same. The man told Gary that he sees her all the time, and she's always wearing the same dress. He's even seen her wandering around his back yard! Who she is, is anyone's guess, as there are hundreds of tombstones in the sprawling cemetery, including one dating back to the Revolutionary War. But we believe, based on her style of dress, that she was from the Victorian era.

Some of the graves in the subject cemetery were relocated from the old burial ground that used to be behind the Dr. Gideon Sprague house at 2831 State Highway 11B in Hopkinton. That house, which I wrote about in *Still More Haunted Northern New York*, now belongs to Jared and Maureen McCargar. In 1840, the small, unnamed backyard cemetery could hold no more graves, as it was only "six rods wide" (according to the *Courier & Freeman* in 1909), so the coffins were dug up and "removed to the present grounds below the village," the Hopkinton-Ft. Jackson Cemetery. And we all know what happens when you start moving remains from place to place!

Kendell Farmhouse

Lake Luzerne

Around 1890, a farmhouse five miles from the community of Lake Luzerne on the southernmost tip of the Adirondack Park was abandoned by the Kendell family. Twenty years later, even though the house had remained deserted that entire period of time, locals began hearing organ music from within its decrepit walls as they passed by, day or night. They avoided what they believed to be their community's haunted house (every community has one) and called its invisible organist "the spook." Many people went so far as to walk on the far side of the road when it became necessary to pass the property. But a few brave souls were forced to confront the alleged specter when they were contracted to cut pine logs on the Kendell estate.

According to the 1913 New Year's Eve edition of Potsdam's *Courier & Freeman*, a lumber crew chief named Frank Huntington had rushed from the Kendell place to Lake Luzerne "in a highly nervous condition," complaining that "the ghostly organist had [just] given him and his men an evening concert, and every man on the job was ready to quit." Can you imagine how the whole lot of them must have felt hearing music they knew was not of this world?

Huntington explained that he had gone to the well for water when he heard what sounded like an organ.

> I thought it was funny anybody should be playing an organ [out in the middle of nowhere] and could not imagine where they could be and decided to hustle around and find out about it. I could not locate it at first, but finally I stepped around in front of the house and listened.

And that's when it hit him square between the eyes that the elders of the community had always said the Kendell place was haunted; so haunted, in fact, that nobody had been able to live in it for twenty years. Huntington continued:

> Believe me, it gave me a chill as I came to the fact that that organ serenade came from the chambers of the partly tumbled down house. I listened about five minutes, and then I went back to the camp and called the boys. We went all through the house and called several times, but no one answered. That was enough for me. There wasn't a soul there, but the music kept right on. It was kinda creepy.

That's it? Just "kinda creepy"? And this from a man who allegedly rushed to the nearest populated area in a state of near-panic! Well, it's good to see that our descriptive terms for paranormal phenomena haven't changed much in a hundred years. Kinda creepy, indeed. The lumber crew chief continued his narrative, describing the sound he and his men had heard:

> It wasn't any regular tune that I ever heard. It must have been one of the old masterpieces. It sounded like somebody was just letting his hands kind of roam up and down the keys.

With an invisible organist playing an invisible organ, is it any wonder the homestead remained abandoned after the Kendells left? And can you blame them for leaving?

The Glass-Topped Coffin

Dannemora

Gently close the little eyes,
Fold the tiny hands so dear,
Put the casket safe away,
Little Hattie is not here.
Treasured tresses from her brow,
Memories guarded by our love,
Still are ours, and these our all;
Little Hattie is above…

Plattsburgh Sentinel, (undated) 1884

As a result of widespread demands for improved prison conditions by local citizens, prison staff, and inmates following the prison riots of 1929, the 1930s marked a decade of new construction and renovations at the Clinton Prison (now the Clinton Correctional Facility in Dannemora). A new powerhouse was essential to the overhaul and expansion of the prison, but construction of the facility required the relocation of the Dannemora Community United Methodist Church Cemetery on Clark Street to the northeast corner of St. Joseph's Cemetery on Smith Street. Such a move, the older residents of the community warned at the time, would surely cause the unrest of those souls whose graves were being disturbed. While such dire predictions rarely halt the steady beat of progress, progress certainly has a way of awakening curious spirits, adding credence to the claims of our elders.

In March 1931, an article in the *Lake Placid News* described events that had transpired after workmen "engaged in excavation for the new power plant" uncovered "an iron coffin with a glass lid" that contained the well-preserved body of a child. The article stated that after the disturbance of the grave, things began happening that proved the location had indeed become haunted. A number of watchmen at the plant had "resigned their positions in rapid succession, giving [only] vague reasons for doing so," but everyone knew the unwritten, unspoken reason for their hasty departures. One watchman insisted on carrying a revolver and shotgun with him while on duty, all the while insisting that he wasn't afraid of ghosts—that is, not until the day he was making the required rounds and nearly fell into a pit that had been previously covered with planks. Nobody knew how the planks became "mysteriously removed," but he couldn't shake the warnings of the village elders, and he resigned his post right then and there.

After discussing this news article with the Saranac Town Historian, Jan Couture, I became aware of two discrepancies in the newspaper's account of the incident. First, it inadvertently listed the location of the relocated cemetery and power house as the village of Redford, rather than Dannemora, ten miles away, where it actually occurred. Second, the paper reported that the body was that of a boy, when it was actually that of a young girl with long, dark hair. Ms. Couture's late father-in-law, a "very wise man" named Amos Couture, dug graves for St. Joseph's Church in Dannemora for forty years, so he was well aware of the incident and had shared the details with Jan prior to his passing in September 2008. He said that he hadn't seen the coffin himself, but he had heard that it was glass-topped and that as it was brought up to the surface, the seal broke, and the well-preserved body of a young girl with long dark hair inside of it disintegrated.

Of the fifteen graves that had to be relocated to St. Joseph's Cemetery, only one belonged to a young girl: that of Hattie F. Gay, who died on March 20, 1861, when she was just six years old. But hers wasn't the only grave disturbed. There were others belonging to people who demanded respect in their day, who perhaps felt insulted after death when their remains were dug up and moved. John Parkhurst, his wife, Maria, and two of their sons (ages five and seventeen) were among the families whose graves had been moved. Mr. Parkhurst, according to his

obituary in the *Plattsburgh Sentinel* on August 25, 1882, "was promi-
nently identified with the former business and political history of
Clinton County. He was a man of more than average natural ability and
force of character." Parkhurst was in charge of the "extensive iron works
of the state" before he "finally became Agent and Warden of the
[Clinton] prison…He managed the affairs of the prison with great ability
and the most scrupulous business integrity." Isn't it possible his spirit
felt a bit of angst, having its earthly remains deracinated by the very
institution he had managed so capably while alive? He had every reason
to "have a little fun" with the watchmen, as far as I'm concerned. And
what about the Hookers? The coffins of Phineas and Lydia Hooker were
also moved during the graveyard shuffle, and they were among the first
permanent settlers of Dannemora. While living in a log shack left by
hunters in 1836, the year Dannemora was settled, the couple boarded
and fed miners who had just begun arriving in the area. Lydia, in fact,
was the first female to ever live in the town. Where was the respect for
their remains? And then, of course, there was little Hattie. If she was, in
fact, the child whose remains disintegrated when lifted from their sacred
resting place, she certainly had a reason to be upset.

Whoever it was, the powerhouse ghost apparently grew tired of
scaring the night watchmen and moved on. *Unless…* it simply moved on
down the road to "The House on Flagg Street," widely reported (online)
to be haunted. Rumor has it that the house, not far from the relocated
cemetery, is haunted by the ghost of a little girl (along with those of a man
and a young boy). They say she loves music, and you can hear her singing...

Evans Mills Rescue Squad

Evans Mills

The first time the garage door to the ambulance bay opened in the middle of the night just moments before an emergency call came in, the EMTs at the Evans Mills Rescue Squad station thought it was a fluke—a timely coincidence, if you will. The next time, they had one of those "hmmm…" moments. By the third time it happened, they realized it couldn't be just another helpful coincidence, but it might well be a helpful *ghost*.

The Evans Mills Volunteer Rescue Squad was formed in 1980. Originally housed elsewhere, they moved into their current headquarters at 8733 Factory Street (County Route 46) in 1992 when a brand new building was built to their specifications on a vacant lot. The members of the squad serve the community and surrounding towns commendably, with each bringing his or her own unique background and experience into the mix.

In 2008, Chief Leah Milot spoke to me about the incidents that have led many of them to believe that their building is haunted, although by whom, they can't say. They were told that their property had, over the years since the 1800s, housed a carriage house, a dance hall, a hotel, and a livery. An 1864 map of the village shows Factory Street being called "Bebee Street;" it also shows a hotel on the corner of Factory and Willow called the A.A. Steele Hotel. At that time, the buildings that stood where today's rescue squad building now stands were simply labeled "W. Sh." and "H. Sh.," which tells us nothing, other than that someone had in fact occupied that location.

According to Leah, "We have many stories from many different members," and their spectral guests seem to especially enjoy picking on new recruits. Leah has experienced a number of paranormal incidents herself, like the time when an ambulance in the garage actually started itself up at around two or three in the morning. Sure, the keys are left in the rigs so the crew doesn't run the risk of having to search for them in an emergency, but someone still had to manually rotate the key in the ignition to start the vehicle. Leah went out to the ambulance bay, shut off the engine, looked around to make sure there were no intruders, and returned back inside. No sooner had she gotten there than an emergency call came in. Apparently, their helpful ghost was trying to save the squad every valuable second.

A male apparition has been seen a number of times looking through the window of the door between the ambulance bay and the common area. Upon investigation, nobody is ever found. Leah described what she saw as the face of an older gentleman in his seventies or eighties— a very clear, distinct face. He was obviously tall, considering how high up on the window his face appeared, with gray hair, a mustache, and a scruffy beard. The apparition remained still, just looking in the window, and then it was gone; others have seen a similar ghostly visage. But usually the ambulance bay ghost appears as nothing more than a shadow darting past the door's window.

There is also a female apparition that haunts the women's quarters. Or at least the squad members believe it's a female, because it restricts its activity to that area. But I imagine a male apparition would enjoy hanging out in the women's area as well! Whatever the gender, this ghost flushes the toilet at random times when nobody is anywhere near it. (Now, if the seat were found left up, we'd be able to determine with certainty what gender the ghost is!) The door in the women's dorm room has been seen opening, then pausing for a moment before closing slowly—the way a door would react when an actual person walks into or out of a room. Squad members have ruled out the possibility that this is caused by another door in the building opening or being slammed shut. Nothing they do (other than physically opening and closing the door) ever results in the particular movement they've witnessed.

While the ambulance bay and women's sleeping quarters seem to experience the most paranormal activity, footsteps and voices have been heard throughout the premises. The thermostat sometimes inexplicably shoots up to seventy-five degrees without anyone touching it, and the television changes channels when nobody is even near the remote. One former EMT said he and others believed there were two ghosts: one is quiet and the other, pretty rowdy. He said, "The hell-raiser seems to act up every time the [calm] one is not around." Apparently, the calm one wasn't there when Leah was reading the first draft of this story about the ghost. She said, "As I finished reading your draft, we heard something in the kitchen area fall." Such is the norm at the rescue squad building.

While some might speculate that the ghost or ghosts are former members or patients who have died in the rigs, I believe they may be people who used to live or work on the property long before the squad building was built and that they are attached to the property itself, rather than to the current building. It'll be interesting to see if the upcoming renovations stir anything up. Spirits are inherently curious beings and seem to come out of the woodwork as soon as work gets under way...literally.

Pine Grove Cemetery Revisited

Massena

Pine Grove #1 Cemetery on Beach Street in Massena has become quite the darling of haunted graveyards. First there was the story of Dragon Obretenoff from my second book, *More Haunted Northern New York*. He starred in the story of a ghost that dared a woman on a leisurely evening stroll across the grounds to "turn around." His unsuspecting victim understandably declined the challenge, so we will never know what the specter looked like, but we have every reason to presume that it was Dragon, since his was the name being discussed when those two words were uttered by an unknown presence, and it happened right near his tombstone, at the rear of the cemetery on the farthest road back.

A few years ago, when the Shadow Chasers were investigating Pine Grove, they set up some stationary equipment in that very location at the back of the cemetery before pairing off and going in opposite directions. It wasn't long before a couple of local cops showed up on their nightly patrol. Little did they know they were about to walk into a ghost trap of sorts. Phil Creighton had placed a digital voice recorder (DVR) with an audio amplifier on a tripod. The device looks like a small, clear satellite dish; with it, one could theoretically hear ghostly chatter through earphones from all the way across the graveyard. That night, however, instead of ghostly chatter, Phil captured something completely unexpected—the voices of a couple of police officers who were circling around the device and asking each other what it was. Phil was certainly reading them loud and clear (and was probably stifling a grin) as he made his way back and whipped out his ID badge to prove he was a paranormal investigator. With that, one of the cops said, "You should be here at 3 A.M. if you wanna really catch something." The policeman proceeded to tell him about two officers who were on routine patrol near the cemetery one night when their radio went "all funky." The frequency scrolled all the way up and all the way down, and the same thing happened to two more officers on patrol near the cemetery several days later. Before the officers left Phil to complete his investigation for the night, one added that she had seen "shadow people" going through the cemetery. It wouldn't be long before Phil, Kate, and the others would understand what she meant.

The next night, the Shadow Chasers returned to Pine Grove, and it proved to be far more exciting than the night before—which is not to downplay the excitement generated when the police had shown up. Right off the bat, the freshly-charged batteries on the camcorder died, much to the dismay of the camera operator. Then, two members of the team were joking about the *Ghost Hunters* show on television, saying how funny it was to see the stars of that show actually running after ghosts, when all of a sudden, they both heard a loud "Psst!" in their ears, at the same time Phil's static monitor blasted an identical static sound. And while all that was going on, other members of the group reported sounds of someone chasing them along the dirt pathways. Cofounder Kate Heuser and another female team member became suddenly nauseated— a sign of exposure to high electromagnetic fields, which are known to cause lightheadedness, nausea, and dizziness. In fact, the entire group experienced nausea to some degree, but they managed to continue their investigation.

Phil recalled looking toward the end of the road at the back of the cemetery, where his attention was drawn toward a streetlamp that seemed to pulsate from bright to dim. As he drew closer, he made out the silhouette or shadow of a person, but there was no actual person any-where in sight. The shadow suddenly darted from under the light toward the cemetery, and the streetlamp immediately brightened. Another mem-ber of the team joined Phil just as the shadow ran back, and they both watched, mesmerized, as the figure darted to and fro, as if toying with its audience. Phil called the entire group over, but the shadow decided to play shy. Only when it had an audience of just one or two would it put on a show. Not only could they see the phantom, they could also hear it

Misty figure on left stepping onto road at cemetery.

make a *swoosh* sound as it passed them (so you know it had to be fast). Phil suggested that it was feeding off his group's energy fields, because the longer they stood around watching it, the faster the entity seemed to become. It was obviously depleting the energy from the streetlamp as well—as indicated by the flickering and pulsating of the light.

A photograph taken right next to Dragon Obretenoff's stone showed what appeared to be an apparition of a man walking toward the road from the gravestones. The misty shape looks vaguely (as ghost photos do) like the side angle of a man's upper and lower body. Is this the shadow person they've dubbed "Arthur"? Or is it Dragon, still waiting for someone to "turn around" and face him?

LeRay Mansion

Fort Drum

On Halloween Day in 2008, WWNY-TV featured a story about the LeRay Mansion at Fort Drum, long rumored to be haunted. Producer Mike Boyce interviewed Dr. Laurie Rush, Cultural Resources Program Manager, for the piece. Dr. Rush provided Boyce and the cameraman with a tour of the site, complete with ghost stories for each stop along the way. In the dining room, where such distinguished guests as President James Monroe and Governor Dewitt Clinton once dined, today's guests tell of chairs moving inexplicably. In the staircase leading to the second floor, phantom children frolic gleefully on the brightly-colored Brussels carpeting. Dr. Rush recalled a little boy's encounter with these child ghosts, as reported by the boy's mother. She and the others in her group were preparing to depart when her young son reminded her to say goodbye to the children. Since he was the only child there, she asked him which children he was talking about. When he told her he meant the children he had been playing with, his mother and the other women realized that, come to think of it, he had seemed almost as if he was playing with someone they didn't see. Furthermore, some of them recalled feeling a slight, nearly-imperceptible movement brushing against them during their stay, touching them at just about child's height.

The bedrooms on the second floor seem particularly active, so much so that cleaning crews have requested different assignments to avoid the possibility of having to face the unknown. In this case, the unknown is a baby that is heard, but not seen. The crying infant is believed to be Sigit, James LeRay's granddaughter, since she was the only infant known to have died on the property. The basement, which once housed the kitchen where servants made meals, has also seen its share of stories. Guests have told Dr. Rush of the door opening on its own. A woman named Anne who works in the office of Cultural Resources posted an article online called "The Slightly Haunted LeRay Mansion at Fort Drum" in which she tells of a brief visit to the basement in search of its alleged ghosts. But all they left with was a funny feeling or sixth sense, which sometimes is our best indication as to whether or not a place is haunted. Others familiar with the house have heard footsteps or seen vague figures in the windows when nobody should be inside. In such an old, historic home as this, paranormal activity would be expected.

James Donatien LeRay de Chaumont, the original owner of the mansion, came from a family of French nobility. His father, Jacques, befriended Benjamin Franklin during the Revolutionary War and gave him a Paris home, where he stayed for nine years. The senior LeRay had also helped finance the war when James was just a young man—thus instilling in his son's mind a spirit of independence and sympathy for the fledgling nation. In the late 1700s, primarily because of his family's acquaintance with Franklin (and the fact that LeRay needed to recoup the money his father spent helping Americans), James LeRay purchased more than six hundred thousand acres of land in Northern New York to parcel off and sell to Quakers and immigrants. In 1806, he dispatched a friend to Pine Plains (now Fort Drum) to find a suitable piece of prop-erty on which to build a home for himself. When the first house burned to the ground, it was replaced by the current LeRay Mansion around 1827. The white, Georgian-style mansion has three-foot-thick, solid stone walls, making it far more enduring than its predecessor. Originally, there were servants' quarters, a chapel, an ice house, French gardens, a park, a land office, farm buildings, a large barn, a man-made pond, the farm manager's quarters, and even what LeRay liked to call his "spy house." Journalist Edward Hungerford, who wrote columns for Doubleday, Page & Company's *Country Life in America* periodical between 1901 and 1917, called the LeRay Mansion of the early twen-tieth century "Old France in young America!" Of the so-called spy house, he said:

From the back of the building, [an unobstructed expanse of lawn] leads through an artificial clearing to the vista of the tiny lake that LeRay created more than a hundred years ago. Here, close by the water, was what he delighted to call his spy-house, a small octagonal building in which he was wont to ascend and from its observatory watch through a spy-glass the doings of his villagers in the small town which he laid out…

Sadly, there was also a need for an onsite burial ground, which may have some bearing on this story. The only member of the LeRay family that was buried on the property was James LeRay's granddaughter, Sigit, the baby daughter of his own beloved daughter, Theresa de Gouvello, for whom he named the Village of Theresa. Sigit was only fifteen months old when she died of smallpox at the estate and was buried near the formal pond. Today, the heiress toddler's tombstone still remains in the woods of the LeRay property. Hungerford's article, which told of many paths running through the property, mentioned her gravesite. He said, "One path [led] to an opening in the wood which holds a few half-forgotten graves. One of these is the final resting place of LeRay's little granddaughter." Hungerford added that the child's mother, Theresa, had married in the LeRay Mansion and that:

>…in one of these tiny old groves, her infant daughter was baptized, on a pleasant afternoon in August 1817. A huge boulder—you still can identify it—was transformed by candles, crucifix, and fair linen into an altar. The summer sun broke through the branches of the trees and danced upon the greensward. And here, the one member of the LeRay family who was destined never to leave America was christened; to be buried a little later, within a short stone's throw…

Little Sigit was not the only person to have died on the estate, however. Others have died of old age, and at least one man was accidentally killed (or murdered). Some 155 years ago, a farm manager shot and killed a man lurking in the early-morning mist on the grounds of the estate. When questioned by the police, the farm manager claimed he had been hunting and thought he was shooting a red fox, but it turned out to be an apparent trespasser on the property. The tragedy was deemed an accident, and the shooter was let off the hook. Nobody ever learned why the deceased had come to the mansion. Perhaps he was interested in purchasing some land from the land baron, LeRay. Is that poor, unfortunate soul now among the mysterious figures occasionally seen (but never found) inside the mansion by security guards on their rounds? A sudden, overwhelming sense of fear has gripped more than one individual while visiting the mansion. Are they sensing the residual energy of the intruder the moment before his suspicious death when he realized he was about to be shot? Or do people pick up on the pain Theresa surely felt while she helplessly watched her baby die of smallpox? Many raw human emotions have been felt at the LeRay Mansion in the past two centuries, and such intense feelings from past incidents often lead to hauntings.

The LeRays owned the mansion until 1840, when it was sold to Jules Rene Payen, a merchant of Dijon, France. Mrs. Julia Phelps, the daughter of Jules Payen and widow of William Phelps, died at the mansion in 1912 at the age of eighty-four. She was just twelve when her family purchased the house, so she had lived there almost her entire life. Her granddaughter, Mabel, married Frederick Anderson in 1900; by the late 1920s, Mabel was the only surviving Payen family member still living at the mansion. Her husband, according to the Hungerford article, had "vast pride in the mansion and its surrounding estate…[and] labored hard to maintain it, carefully watching and replacing every decaying brick or stone or timber in the old house." Clearly, he put his heart and soul into the place while he lived there. Does he still watch over it from the Other Side, making sure the estate is well-kept? This, too, is a common reason for haunting—the desire to see that a property continues to be cared for properly or that a business continues to prosper.

Today, the Directorate of Community Activities holds formal events and celebrations of a military nature at LeRay Mansion. Along with the Department of Cultural Resources, the Directorate works to preserve and manage the historic district encompassing the mansion, which was placed on the National Register of Historic Places in 1974. The district includes the original mansion, chapel, slave quarters, land office, and farm manager's cottage (from which the fatal shot was fired long ago). LeRay Mansion is also available by reservation for officers and dignitaries, but according to an Army officer's wife I spoke to, there are people she knows who refuse to go back into the mansion because of paranormal experiences they've had there.

Fort Ticonderoga

Fort Ticonderoga

The dead are everywhere!
The mountain-side, the plain, the wood profound,
All the wide earth, the fertile and the fair,
Is one vast burial-ground!

From Angels' Whispers, by Daniel C. Eddy, D.D. (1881)

The French built Fort Ticonderoga (then called Fort Carillon) during the French and Indian War just above a narrow waterway connecting Lake Champlain to Lake George, and the St. Lawrence River Valley to the Hudson River Valley. Due to its strategic location, the fort saw four coup d'états in just two decades. The 460 acres at Fort Ticonderoga are densely blanketed with unmarked graves, which explains why it now harbors hundreds of restless spirits. To give you perhaps a better visual, read what a visitor to the fort in 1854 told the *Daily Gazette* (Janesville, Wisconsin) on August 25 of that year:

> Two weeks ago, this day, I stood for the first time in my life in the ancient graveyard of old Fort Ticonderoga. Here and there in quite regular order could be traced the narrow hollows, made by the earth caving in, and filling the space once occupied by the mortal remains of some poor soldier. Here and there, in rows almost hid by the grass, could be seen the rude, unfinished and unlettered head and foot stones

which once marked their resting place…Indeed here one is alone with the dead of one hundred years ago. Hundreds, yes thousands, lie about this neglected graveyard; a few of whom died natural deaths, but the great majority came to their end in an untimely hour, in the unholy strife of battle…

Construction of Fort Carillon began in 1755. Two years later, the sturdy stone fort was open and ready for business—the business of controlling the southern part of Lake Champlain to prevent the British from gaining access. Because of the French victory in the attack (from Fort Carillon) on Fort William Henry during the French and Indian War in 1757 and the Battle of Carillon (when 16,000 British troops were miraculously defeated by just 4,000 French defenders) in 1758, the fort enjoyed a short-lived reputation of being invincible—and so the legends began.

Duncan Campbell was a Scottish Highlander of the 42nd Regiment of Foot (the legendary Black Watch) of the British Army who was killed in the Battle of Carillon. Three years earlier, Campbell had invited a blood-soaked stranger into his castle in Inveraray, Argyll, Scotland, one night, unaware that the man had just murdered his (Campbell's) cousin (though many sources say it was his brother). The *New York Times* ran a story written by John Walker Harrington on July 2, 1922, called "Fort Ticonderoga's International Ghost Story" that describes the incident in great detail. The killer, unaware that the man from whom he was seeking shelter was related to his victim, told him, "I have just killed a man and am being pursued…For God's sake, hide me. Swear on your dirk not to give me up." In a split-second decision, Campbell unwittingly gave the solemn pledge to the stranger and hid him in his cellar. Just then, the search party arrived and gave Campbell the grim news about the death of his relative. Rather than direct the men to the cellar, he pleaded ignorance when asked if he had seen the killer. Moments after the men left, Campbell was visited for the first of three times by the ghost of his murdered kin, Donald Campbell, who said: "Inverawe! Inverawe! Blood has been shed! Shield not the murderer!"

When Campbell told the killer in his cellar what he had seen, he was quickly reminded of his pledge to never give him up. But Campbell could not bear to shelter the man in his own castle, so instead, he took him under cover of darkness to a secret cave where he could hide out. The spirit of Donald Campbell was not pleased, for it appeared to Campbell a second time that night, repeating the plea from his first visit. The next morning, Campbell went to the cave, only to find that the fugitive had escaped. With a heavy heart, he returned to the castle. That night, for the third and final time, the ghost of Donald appeared to him with a cryptic goodbye: "Farewell, farewell, till we meet at Ticonderoga!" Campbell had never heard of such a place, and neither had most people—especially those overseas—for it was an Iroquois word meaning "the junction of two waterways," and the fort had not yet been built in the small New York State village.

While he never forgot the dire warning, it wasn't until 1756 that Campbell first heard the word "Ticonderoga" spoken by someone other than a ghost. That year, the Black Watch, to which Major Campbell belonged, was dispatched to New York and told that they were to attack Louisburg, Crown Point, and...*Ticonderoga*.

History would soon prove the ghostly premonition true. The Black Watch suffered many casualties in the Battle of Carillon in July 1758. More than three hundred Highlanders perished on the grounds of Fort Ticonderoga that day—many of them bayoneted to death. As for Campbell, he was "wounded by a slug from artillery in his right arm," but the injury was not considered serious. Yet, as if in some self-fulfilling prophecy—for he had insisted to his fellow officers that he would die at Ticonderoga—he succumbed to blood poisoning from his battle injury just nine days later. What's more, while the deadly Battle of Carillon was taking place, several witnesses reported that an accurate depiction of the battle scene was simultaneously replicated in the skies over his beloved Inveraray Castle in Scotland. A man named William Hart was walking around the grounds of the Campbell estate that day when he saw it, as did his servant and a friend. In the sky was a vision of a battle scene depicting Highland forces attacking French troops behind fortifications. The Highlanders, though gallantly fighting, were repeatedly overwhelmed by musket fire and bayonets in the aerial apparition. Later that same day, two young women arrived at the castle claiming that they, too, had seen a horrifying battle in the sky. Of course, none of the five witnesses could possibly have known a battle involving their own kin was taking place at the very same time of their vision. It would be several weeks before news of the Battle of Carillon reached the Campbell estate in Scotland.

In 1759, the British captured the fort during the Battle of Ticonderoga and renamed their prize, aptly, "Fort Ticonderoga." In 1775, Ethan Allen, Benedict Arnold, and the Green Mountain Boys of Vermont paid a surprise visit to the fort and seized control peacefully from the sleeping British garrison in an event that marked the first offensive victory of the Revolutionary War. It was then that Anthony Wayne, a United States Army general, was dispatched to Fort Ticonderoga to command the distressed forces there. Wayne's fiery personality and military feats would earn him the moniker of "Mad Anthony." He was as cocky and heartless in the romance arena as he was on the battlefield, but there were always women impressed with his military (and other) prowess wherever he went. He would love them and leave them—never anything more. But that cavalier philosophy was unbearable to one woman he courted.

When Mad Anthony first arrived at Fort Ticonderoga during the Revolutionary War, he quickly familiarized himself with the ladies of the area by hosting a dinner party on the premise of celebrating his arrival. Nancy Coates was a local widow who was intimately familiar (if you know what I mean) with the soldiers. She happened to be serving at the party that night and quickly caught the eye of the general, who had no doubt been informed of her reputation. Yes, she would do. But then the beautiful, young, *unattainable* Penelope Haynes walked by, and from that moment on, Mad Anthony could think of no other. Even as he courted Nancy Coates, he was lusting for Penelope, the daughter of a rich Vermont landowner. One day General Washington ordered Mad Anthony to protect the women in the vicinity of the fort from the British, as attacks were escalating. When he returned to Fort Ticonderoga that fateful day, Penelope would accompany him (after all, she was a woman to protect, too). Nancy, meanwhile, was already at the fort, eagerly awaiting the general's return. She asked if anyone had seen Mad Anthony, and some thoughtless women jokingly told her they heard he was bringing home his young bride. Disbelieving, Nancy turned to a soldier nearby and asked if that was the truth, and he played along and said it was. Stunned and heartbroken, Nancy wandered aimlessly along the footpaths through the brush, contemplating her next move. Finally, she heard the familiar sound of the general returning and ran to the trail to meet him, praying that what she had heard wasn't true. But it was…or at least it appeared to be. There, before her bloodshot eyes, were the general and Penelope, clearly enjoying each others' company too much to notice her standing there. With that, Nancy Coates turned, walked into Lake Champlain, and deliberately drowned herself. Her body was eventually found floating near the shoreline by soldiers who were fishing in the area. Ever since then, a woman (believed to be the ghost of Nancy Coates) can be heard sobbing in the vicinity, and reports of an apparition drifting along the shore of Lake Champlain and wandering around the grounds of the old fort persist.

In 1777, the British returned to the fort, more determined than ever to take it back. They climbed to the top of Mt. Defiance, armed with cannons they had every intention of using, and threatened to rain cannonballs down upon Fort Ticonderoga. Realizing the futility of their efforts, the Americans abandoned the fort, leaving it once again to the British. That year marked the last of the military engagements at Ticonderoga. By 1780, the importance of the fort for strategic purposes during wartime had waned, and it was wholly abandoned.

In 1820, the ruins of the old fort were purchased by William Ferris Pell, who built a home overlooking the lake called The Pavilion, which would become a hotel for tourists visiting the national historic treasure. Stephen and Sarah Gibbs Thompson Pell acquired the fort in 1908, restored it, and opened it to the public in 1909. According to a history of the fort compiled by Dr. Bara H. Loveland in 2006, the Pells' grandson, John Bigelow Pell Loveland, recalled hearing strange knocking in his guestroom at the Pavilion and fearing that a ghost had followed him from the dungeon of the fort, where he often played as a child while spending summers there. He ended up moving into new sleeping quarters when the knocking became too unnerving. Loveland also recalled a family friend named Lady Jean Campbell telling him that she once saw a headless apparition at the Pavilion when she lived on the expansive grounds of the fort.

Fort Ticonderoga was designated a non-profit educational historic site in 1931. In 1960, the restored eighteenth-century fort became a National Historic Landmark. Today, it's a privately-owned attraction that includes a well-stocked museum, store, and onsite restaurant. The Pavilion overlooking the King's Garden is in the process of being restored for the public to enjoy. The museum's cleaning staff admit that they have found objects in locked display cases that were somehow moved around in the night. People continue to report seeing red and white orbs floating around the compound, an ethereal feminine form running along the trails, and redcoats in the old barracks. And one can, on occasion, still hear the mournful sobbing of a woman scorned more than two hundred years ago.

Picketville Ghost

Parishville

What began as a familiar stroll into the quaint little village of Parishville by a young woman in the late 1800s resulted in that community's own enduring ghost tale, one that's lasted more than a hundred years. In her June 2, 1987, column, Helen Condon, the Parishville and Hopkinton correspondent of the *Courier & Freeman*, shared the story with readers.

It began long ago at the residence of Mr. Warner, a reverend who offered sermons at the local church and ran a small farm on Picketville Road, several miles south of Parishville proper. According to legend and Mrs. Condon's interpretation of it, the girl Mr. Warner had hired to work on his farm set out for the village early one summer evening to run some errands. She was last seen in the vicinity of the Eagle Hotel, which was located in the middle of town near the barbershop and several stores. What she was shopping for has been lost to history, but it was reported that the last person the girl encountered was a teamster hired to transport whisky to the southern part of the state. The girl never returned to the Warner's home and was never seen or heard from again. The teamster also disappeared unexpectedly the night that the girl went missing, fueling speculation that he had murdered her and skipped town.

About a year later, Condon said that road crews on Picketville Road found the remnants of a woman's dress that matched the one the girl had been wearing when she disappeared. It seemed even more likely at that point that she had, in fact, been killed. The icing on the cake (of that theory), in the absence of any other evidence, was when an apparition believed to be the murdered young woman appeared near the spot where

59

the fabric was found…and continued appearing for the next fifty years. Over time, the sightings became fewer and farther between, but when they did occur, they were enough to turn skeptics into believers. One, a Mr. Lucas, said he saw a young, silent woman from a distance of about forty feet. But after a few seconds and a few more careful steps toward her, the solid-appearing figure vanished into thin air—just as she had seemingly done at the tragic end of her life.

Phantom Bridge

Ausable Chasm

I've heard of phantom planes, phantom trains (like the legendary Lincoln ghost train), and even an occasional phantom building. These are objects that no longer exist, yet have been seen, heard, or (as in the case of the phantom building) even visited. Inevitably, they appear and disappear mysteriously as each hapless victim stumbles upon them. Such sightings might be residual hauntings, or they could be psychic impressions sensed by certain individuals depicting events or structures that once existed at that location. In cases such as the following, a phantom structure appears at just the right moment, serves its purpose, and then vanishes. It helps when your mode of transportation when this happens is a horse, as their intuitive ability allows them to sense impressions left on the environment more acutely than humans.

In 1897, the *Plattsburgh Sentinel* ran a story called "A Legend of the Ausable: A Horseman Drove across the Ghost of a Bridge." The article originally ran in the *Chicago Times-Herald*, and it recalled a story that had occurred one hundred years prior. A man named Max Morgan, according to that story, rode into town on his horse one night, found the old wooden bridge over the chasm that he had helped build years earlier when he lived nearby, and rode across it to a tavern he knew about on the other side. The tavern keeper, making friendly conversation, asked the unfamiliar traveler if he'd had any trouble finding the inn on such a dark, starless night. After all, even the regulars really had to know where they were going to find it in the dark. Morgan replied matter-of-factly that it was no problem at all, for he remembered the path to the High Bridge (as it was called when it was built in 1793) so well that he could have found it blindfolded! Silence fell upon the tavern, as customers within earshot waited with bated breath to see how this interesting exchange would end up.

The innkeeper stared at Morgan for a moment, sizing him up, and when he realized the man was serious, he pointed out a minor detail that would make Morgan's claim impossible. The High Bridge, which had been made of gigantic Norway pine logs and planks, had been washed away years earlier. It had only survived twenty years. By the time Morgan returned to town and found his way to the tavern, all that remained of the bridge was a *single*, narrow log (stringer) spanning the deep, deep chasm. It would be virtually impossible for a horse carrying a man to trot across the chasm while balancing on a single log on a night of utter darkness. It would be virtually impossible even in broad daylight. Horses can't trot gingerly across a single stringer (and don't they have a fear of heights, anyway?). An unwilling horse would surely shy sideways at the precipice.

But Morgan insisted that even though he hadn't actually seen the bridge in the dark, he had clearly *heard* his horse's hooves trotting across the familiar planking—as well as the sound of churning water a hundred and twenty-five feet below! Since neither man believed the other, a bet was waged as to the bridge's existence, and it was decided that they (and practically all of the townspeople, as it turned out) would meet at the site of the old High Bridge the next morning. John Hilliard, the reporter who wrote the piece for the *Chicago Times-Herald* said, "Sure enough, in the soft sand of the road, there were footprints of a horse, and the trail led from the stringer across the chasm up to the tavern porch." One brave (or foolish, depending on your point of view) young man volunteered to walk across the chasm on the stringer to determine if there were, in fact, hoofprints leading onto the stringer at the other side. Sure enough, there were.

So it was true. Morgan and his horse had crossed the deep, deadly chasm on a single log, on a night so dark that they couldn't see what lay ahead (or below), with Morgan assuming that they were crossing the bridge he had helped to build years earlier. Horrified at the realization of his own unintentional, death-defying stunt, Morgan began shaking uncontrollably, and the shakes lasted the rest of his life, according to the article. What's more, his hair changed from jet black to snow white in the blink of an eye, a phenomenon often mentioned in literature but not supported by science. The scientific explanation is that the condition occurs when a sudden, extreme shock causes a person's hair to begin growing in white, so it would take quite some time before someone would get a full head of white hair. However, numerous historical accounts describe the condition as occurring much faster, with a full head of hair (even a woman's long, dark hair) turning white almost instantly—as allegedly happened to poor Max Morgan.

Photo courtesy of Wikimedia Commons.

Ausable Chasm, 1907.

Regarding the legend of Max Morgan, the Ausable Chasm website states, "They say that angels were on hand to carry him to the other side." Better the other side of the bridge than *the* Other Side!

Sackets Harbor Battlefield

Sackets Harbor

The Battle of Sackets Harbor during the War of 1812 occurred on May 29, 1813, and resulted in a large number of fatalities, both American and British. Various sources report that anywhere between 69 and 172 men were killed in battle that day, and many more were taken prisoner or became missing in action. One American taken prisoner by the British was dragged off into the woods by Indians who then killed and scalped him—and not necessarily in that order.

Today, the remaining structures at the Battlefield, including the Commandant's House and the Lieutenant's House, now used as the orientation center, have been carefully restored. Visitors can enjoy guided or self-guided tours on trails marked with signs and view exhibits in the historic old buildings. In the summer months, the 1813 battle is reenacted by volunteers wearing period clothing. But who needs reenactment when you can hear and see the real thing?

As with most former battlegrounds, the one at Sackets Harbor is now quite haunted, to put it mildly. It's not often that I come across a location that runs the gamut of paranormal activity, encompassing everything you can imagine—EVPs, orbs, apparitions, residual hauntings, reciprocal hauntings, energy drainage, and equipment malfunction. You name it, I've seen or heard about it happening at the Battlefield.

That's why I didn't hesitate in October 2008 when WPBS-TV invited my family and I—along with the Shadow Chasers—to accompany their bus tour to the Battlefield and other haunted locations I've written about in the Watertown area as part of their "Folklore and Frost" event.

Most of the thirty-some individuals from that first night's tour had already boarded the bus, but a handful of us couldn't pull ourselves away. We remained on the grounds near the officers' quarters, too absorbed in the task at hand to call it a night yet—regardless of how late the hour. We were in the middle of a lively discussion about how active things were suddenly becoming, when Kate Heuser, cofounder of the Shadow Chasers, came running up to us breathlessly in the dark, whispering as loudly as one can whisper, "We got it. We got it!" "It," as it turned out, was a woman's small voice on the battlefield saying, "Help me," and a man's voice interrupting, making it clear he didn't want the woman to be helped. There was also the faint sound of scuffling and footsteps. Kate held out the digital voice recorder (DVR) so cofounder, Phil Creighton, could play it back. We all leaned in closer, staring at Phil's hand while listening carefully to the recording. Suddenly it went silent, and in that jaw-dropping moment, Phil blurted, "No." One look at his face, and I echoed that sentiment.

Even though the recording device requires, as a safety feature, a particular sequence of four or five steps to delete a recording, somehow the EVP we were listening to had been wiped out in the blink of an eye without anyone so much as moving. And it wasn't just that EVP. Every single folder storing EVPs was gone. As disappointing as that was, my spirits were lifted the next morning when we loaded the photographs my daughter Jamie had taken that night onto my computer.

Photo by Leland Farnsworth.

One lone orb—the scalped prisoner in the woods?

Earlier that first night, we all followed Phil and Kate into the woods and fields of the old battleground. When we were far enough removed from the buses and buildings, Kate asked everyone to stand still and be silent for a few moments so that she could make a recording. It was a pretty amazing sight to see thirty people practically holding their breath and freezing in mid-step. But we did it; you could hear a pin drop in the silence. After a couple of attempts to capture EVPs along the trail, we hit the jackpot. Phil turned the volume up so we could all hear the faint popping sound of distant musket fire as well as the unintelligible, muted sounds of men's voices yelling, as if in battle. Most people on the tour were armed with digital cameras—myself and daughter Jamie included. Everyone was capturing orbs and various other anomalies in their photographs, so there was a lot of excitement in the air.

I couldn't wait to get home to see the images we'd captured, because the LCD screen on our camera had gone blank (before the tour), so we couldn't tell what we were getting as we were taking pictures. I knew I would not be disappointed, because Jamie was taking a lot of pictures. Besides getting a number of orbs on film, she had inadvertently taken a photograph (page 68) of what could only be described as an apparition taking form. When she took that photograph, we were standing precisely where the dreaded disappearing-EVP incident took place, as described earlier. A couple of people on the tour, including Phil, had just seen a dark shadow zip across the yard at super-human speed toward a vacant building, and the sighting was followed immediately by the sound of a door closing. Jamie pointed her camera in the direction of the building and snapped a picture. In the photograph, you can see a human-like apparition taking shape precisely between Jamie and the building she was attempting to photograph.

Another photograph that Jamie took appears to be a profile of a skeletal face, and since it took up half the photo, it must have been practically on top of us when she took it. This one was taken as we strolled across the grounds toward the spot described above. Every time one of us got a funny feeling about a particular spot in the darkness, Jamie just snapped a picture. This unconventional method obviously worked for us.

The following weekend my husband, Leland, accompanied me on the tour. Like Jamie, he captured many orbs along the trails, but he also captured

Photo by Jamie Revai.

*Apparition taking shape, just as a shadow was seen
and a door mysteriously closed.*

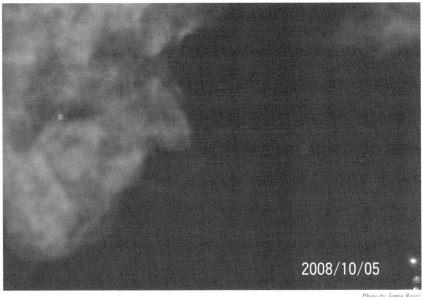

Photo by Jamie Revai.

Skeletal profile of apparition—too close for comfort.

Photo by Leland Farnsworth.

Apparition of soldier with musket.

what appear to be apparitions of soldiers at battle. You can see almost an entire human form looking down and holding a straight, long, musket-like object. Notice the many orbs (no doubt, fallen soldiers) at his feet.

Two more photographs appear to have soldiers in battle (page 70). The first looks like soldiers on horses barreling forward. The second is tremendously-dense spirit mist that (like the other images captured there) was not visible to the naked eye. You can see several long, straight objects in the mist that could be muskets of the soldiers whose apparitions seem to be manifesting in this photo.

Besides my family's photographs, others captured "ribbon energy" at the battlefield, orbs in motion, and various types of spirit energy. One person on the tour pointed out to the others that a red light had somehow come on in one of the vacant houses on the grounds, but a photograph taken a short time earlier shows no sign whatsoever of lighting from within the building. Needless to say, nobody walked away from the bus tours feeling cheated out of experiencing something paranormal at the Sackets Harbor Battlefield.

Photo by Leland Farnsworth.

Apparition of soldiers on horses.

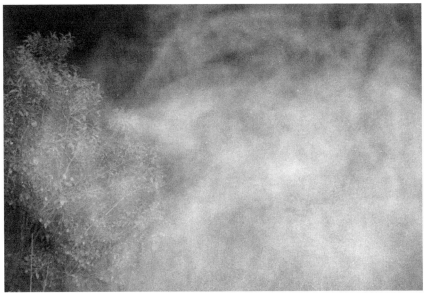

Photo by Leland Farnsworth.

Dense spirit energy of soldiers in battle. Muskets are visible.

Thompson Park

Watertown

Northern New York boasts its very own "mysterious place," according to Frank Joseph's *Sacred Sites: A Guidebook to Sacred Centers and Mysterious Places*. It's the historic Thompson Park in Watertown, which sits smack in the center of the city with entrances off Gotham, Academy, and Franklin Streets. Here, the Thompson Park Conservatory operates the New York State Zoo, and there are also tennis courts, sledding areas, and cross-country ski trails, the Watertown Golf Club, and a pavilion and stairways made of stone. But there is also, according to many believers, a portal (an invisible doorway to the spirit world where spirits come and go with ease) and a rarely-seen vortex believed to be in a grove of trees near the exercise course, golf course, and swimming pool. On a *Strange USA* blog, the founders of Believers of Paranormal and the Spiritual in Watertown reported that they had found the precise location of the elusive vortex, and other individuals and investigators believed that they, too, have stumbled upon it.

A vortex is, by *Encarta's* definition, "a whirling mass of something, especially water or air, that draws everything near it toward its center." In a paranormal sense, the phenomenon can strike either fear or anticipation into those who witness it. Vortices are unpredictable, appearing and disappearing suddenly. When they occur, people have glimpsed, if only for a fleeting moment, buildings or structures from another place and time. Humans have reportedly vanished (in front of witnesses) and resurfaced at a different location seconds or even hours later, disoriented and unable to account for their lost time. It is that characteristic of vortexes that justifiably makes people hesitant to step into them, for fear that they won't return.

I've written about other places believed to contain such mystical features, and usually they seem to be located on sacred sites such as Indian burial grounds, possibly because the Native American seers were able to sense gateways through which their dead could more easily cross over to the Great Spirit. Often, places that are extremely haunted by a number of ghosts are believed to contain portals. Spanky's Diner in Massena comes to mind. There, spirits allegedly told psychic investigators that the diner was a "Grand Central Station," if you will, where spirits could come and go with ease. Perhaps the most famous portals and vortices were found in the Bermuda Triangle, where, for many years in the mid-twentieth century, ships and aircraft disappeared without a trace. Nobody knows for certain what causes these seeming breaches into other dimensions, but the theory suggested in *Sacred Sites* is that they exist where glaciers have deposited unusual energy into the earth in objects such as the stone in the walls at Thompson Park. The object then absorbs and continually releases the unusual energy back into the atmosphere, where it may manipulate the environment in unexpected ways, through features such as vortices and portals. Physical proof of such phenomena can be seen in numerous photographs and videos that depict orbs coming and going, as well as a number of other photographic anomalies.

The particulars of the paranormal incidents which allegedly have occurred at Thompson Park were reported not only in the aforementioned book, but also in regional newspapers including the *Watertown Daily Times* and the *Syracuse Post-Standard*. A number of online sites also mention the park and its other-worldly mysteries. One local resident said on the *Strange USA* website that in the late eighties and early nineties, there was a lot of activity reported, and some of the individuals involved in those particular incidents are too scared to return to the park to this day because of what they witnessed. The individual said that people have seen a large, floating mass drifting across the field on the property, as well as apparitions of a Dutch woman and child. Another resident on a different web site said he had captured mysterious voices on tape, as well as the sound of a horse "clomping on the ground" and snorting. And on *Unsolved Mysteries*, an online repository of all things mysterious, it was said that a feeling of unease often comes over people who are standing near one of the stone walls on the grounds of the park, and that unexplained sounds have been heard and apparitions of a small boy have been seen.

The most common story tells of visitors vanishing into thin air and reappearing elsewhere moments later. The first such incident to receive publicity occurred in the mid-seventies when a man disappeared in plain sight of witnesses as he walked up the hill, away from the group he was with. Twenty minutes later, as the others frantically searched for him, he reappeared behind them, telling them he'd been looking for them, and he had no idea how he had gotten to the bottom of the hill or how long he had been gone. A few years later, the same thing happened, allegedly to one of the members of the original group; she was there with students who reported that she had vanished before their eyes.

In 1901, the year after construction began on the new "City Park on Pinnacle Hill," as it was then known, the *Watertown Daily Times* ran a story saying that a stone balustrade was being built at the top of its summit. Stone steps were also in the process of being "laid up the steep slope of that famous hump of ground," where hundreds of city residents would gather for picnics and sightseeing during the previous century. If the magnetism of Pinnacle Hill is responsible for drawing people near, perhaps it's that same magnetism that occasionally distorts a geographical location's time and space. Whether Thompson Park truly does have a portal or vortex would be difficult to prove, but it does seem possible that, if nothing else, it's haunted, like many historic properties in the North Country. Reports of disembodied voices are common, and the hills and stone walls surely make voices (whether spectral or from the living) sound even more eerie than they otherwise would. Is someone calling out from one dimension to another? When zookeeper Emerson Joyce was mauled and crushed to death by an angry bear at the park in June 1930, did his dying screams remain imprinted on the environment as a residual haunting, like the sound of musket fire from long-ago in Sackets Harbor? There seems to be *something* manipulating energy there. When the Shadow Chasers investigated Thompson Park in October 2008 for a segment on WWNY-TV, they noted "strange fluctuations" in energy fields in the daytime. Seasoned investigator Phil Creighton said that were he taking the same readings at night—a time when energy fields are inherently stronger—they would likely border on the ridiculous.

> While accompanied by Fox News [Watertown], we thoroughly surveyed the park, uncovering a unique grid-like pattern of high EMF [electromagnetic frequency] and RF [radio frequency] spread over the area. Given the readings we were getting in the afternoon, it was likely that the energy pattern was responsible for the "vortex" phenomenon. When someone comes in contact with the high energy bands, it temporarily shorts out their mind, leaving them on auto-pilot for a while (sort of like sleep-walking—somnambulism). The result is that when someone snaps out of this state, they find themselves in a strange area they weren't in before; thus, creating the illusion of traveling a distance without crossing the distance in between.

I contacted the park when I was writing my first book in 2000 to ask for their input on the matter, and the only response I received came from a maintenance employee who said he had never seen or heard anything in all his time there. However, a few days later, I received an unexpected package in the mail from him—old copies of newspaper articles regarding the alleged phenomenon. He may have had reservations about telling me outright what he knew, but in his own subtle way, he provided the affirmation I was looking for.

Old Essex County Courthouse

Elizabethtown

The old Essex County Courthouse at 7551 Court Street *should* be haunted, given its storied, historic past, and a little piece of modern technology may have just recently provided evidence that it is. The handsome building began as a one-story brick courthouse around 1824. The second floor that became the actual courtroom was added in 1843 but was removed in 1880 to create a spacious open chamber with stairs leading to the gallery. In 1888, a wing was added, and the main building was further expanded. Today, the old courthouse no longer holds court, but as the Essex County Government Center, it does house the Board of Supervisors' chambers and the County Manager's office, along with other county offices. It also holds a server room for the Information Systems Department, which I'll get to in a moment. The new courthouse is at the far end of the original courthouse grounds.

One of the most significant tidbits of the old courthouse's history is that in December 1859, the body of abolitionist John Brown was held there overnight while it was in transit to its final resting place at his farm in North Elba, near Lake Placid. Brown was an American abolitionist whose views were considered extreme at the time, since he preferred quick, forceful action to expedite an end to slavery. He was captured by federal forces following his failed Harper's Ferry raid; tried for murder, conspiring with slaves to rebel, and treason to the State of Virginia; and hanged for his crimes. President Lincoln called him a "misguided fanatic," saying he was justly hanged, and others called him the "most controversial of all 19th-century Americans." Historians of today agree that Brown's plight helped kick off the start of the Civil War, and for that reason, many now consider him a martyr. A historical plaque outside of the old County Courthouse marks the spot: "John Brown's Body guarded by local citizens rested in this court house on the night of Dec. 6, 1859, on its way to burial at his home in North Elba." The site is noteworthy, too, because it was an anti-slavery meeting place.

The building was recognized, as courthouses intrinsically are, as a place you didn't want to find yourself being led into in handcuffs and shackles, as was the brutal, nineteenth-century wife killer, Henry Debosnys, whom I've written about extensively in previous books. Debosnys was imprisoned in the Essex County Jail to await his execution before two thousand people who had obtained tickets for the sensational event. His 1883 hanging, the last in the county, occurred in front of the old Essex County Courthouse, and his restless spirit is now believed to haunt the Adirondack History Center Museum where his skull, the noose that strangled him, and a ticket to the hanging are just a few of the items that can be seen in an exhibit devoted entirely to that case. Does Henry's tortured soul also haunt the grounds of the government center complex where his fate was sealed, attempting to disrupt the old seat of justice? One solitary, mysterious incident that occurred at the courthouse in May 2008 seems to indicate he might.

According to the May 19, 2008, public minutes of the Board of Supervisors' Personnel & Administration Committee meeting, a "fiber line problem" was traced to a locked server room in the courthouse where a whip line was found to have been broken, somehow, though nobody had been in that room. According to County Manager and Director of Information Systems, Daniel Palmer:

> ...we have a Charter fiber line that runs from here down to the Public Safety Building, last Sunday it did go down. This is a leased line from Charter Communications, it's monitored 24/7...It turned out that it was a broken whip line and what happens is when your primary connection comes into the building from the connection to a switch, there is a small, thin fiber-optic line that connects from one to the other, and one of them had gotten physically broken. I have no idea how

it got broken in a locked Information Systems Department, in a locked server room, but it did...it was a physically broken whip line.

Later in the meeting, Moriah Town Supervisor, Tom Scozzafava, brought the broken line issue up again, asking if it looked as if it had been done intentionally or, perhaps, like it was vandalism. He quipped, "Do we have ghosts running around the building? If nobody is getting into that room, I mean, is it being investigated?" (He may have been more on the mark than he intended.) Palmer responded, "I don't know how to investigate it, Tom. I honestly don't." Scozzafava asked if there was a camera in that room (there wasn't) and said, "You might want to think about having something in there. How does a line 'just break'?" Palmer said, "Potentially, could a mouse get on there and somehow break the line? Potentially, I guess. But there were no chew marks or anything like that...Maybe it was [about] due to break, but those were all brand new that were just in there. It is a little bit disconcerting to me."

Disconcerting, indeed. It may be nothing at all, but then again, the idea of ghosts running around in a 166-year-old building isn't so far-fetched, especially considering its history. When I asked Mr. Scozzafava about the incident on December 13, 2008, he said, "We never did find out what happened to the line." Maybe those cameras will eventually shed some light on the cunning courthouse culprit.

Hub Theme Cottage

Canton

"There she is!" Those were the words the students and reporters closely huddled around the diminutive woman had been waiting to hear. Three simple words that instilled an immediate reaction of both fear and anticipation, while at the same time confirming an idea each participant had already entertained. There was a woman haunting the building at 1 Lincoln Street on the St. Lawrence University (SLU) campus.

Thirty years ago, two familiar figures in the paranormal field paid a visit to what is now an SLU theme cottage called "The Hub." Ed and Lorraine Warren, the now deceased demonologist and his clairvoyant wife, arrived for a two-day event that included a lecture regarding the cases they had investigated (most notably, the "Amityville Horror") and a walk-through of the property at 1 Lincoln to determine who, if anyone, haunted the storied dorm. Their visit on January 9, 1979, offered insight into the ghost stories associated with the old building, but it also raised questions, such as why was a female apparition seen repeatedly placing an object into the butler's pantry? Did it have to do with unfinished business that kept her spirit earthbound?

The residence in question was built in 1861 for the venerable Dr. John Stebbins Lee, the Principal of the Preparatory Department at the early St. Lawrence University, though some have called him the first president of the school, possibly because most of his obituaries at the time of his death, including one in the *New York Times*, referred to him as such. Regardless, Dr. Lee and his wife, Elmina Bennett, were extremely well-regarded at SLU and in the Canton community, where they raised five children who all went on to find success in Canton and elsewhere (as college presidents, scholars, professors, and educators). One daughter, Florence Lee Whitman, seems to be the target of the ghost stories at 1 Lincoln, even though she's a highly improbable candidate for haunting. The *Cambridge Women's Heritage Project Database* (online) says the legend of Florence's ghost, as promulgated by the last fraternity that occupied the house, was odd, given that Florence had not "died tragically" in her childhood home as the Beta Iota Chapter of Phi Kappa Sigma claimed. In a story about ghosts on the SLU website, the chapter, which was permanently closed in December 2006, said her spirit remained in the house, "a mischievous, teasing wraith." (Someone's been reading too many ghost stories!) In actuality, none of the Lee children died in the Lee House, and Florence, who lived to be 86 years old, died naturally in her home in Cambridge, Massachusetts.

John Stebbins Lee, however, did die at home in September 1902, and Elmina died less than six months later on February 5, 1903, at Florence's home in Cambridge, where she stayed following her husband's passing. Her body was returned to the family home at 1 Lincoln for services before being placed beside her husband's at the Evergreen Cemetery. According to her obituary in the Gouverneur *Free Press* on February 11, 1903:

> She and her husband were residents of Canton from 1859 till the death of the latter in September 1902, and their charming house was a place of delight to the hundreds of students of St. Lawrence University who received there a cordial welcome. Mrs. Lee was a lady of great refinement and sincere kindness, with a heart ever young and a deep interest in young people…The funeral was held at the old home of the family in Canton…

For several years, the Sigma Alpha Epsilon fraternity occupied the Civil War era building before selling it to J.H. Powers for his family of nine. A 1924 *Commercial Advertiser* article says Dr. Lee and his wife, Elmina Bennett, had planned the design of the spacious home in 1859, and it was built under their direction. In fact, it was built so well that, when it was moved on skids in 1924 to the rear of the lot where it now stands on the corner of Park and Lincoln, its structural integrity remained sound. The Powers family lived there from 1924 until 1928, when they were forced to sell the home due to financial difficulties. It was then that St. Lawrence University acquired it for occupancy by the Gamma Sigma Rho fraternity, according to an article in the Canton Commercial Advertiser of March 6, 1928, called "University Buys the Old Lee House—Built by the First President of the College." Throughout the remainder of the twentieth century and into the twenty-first, the old Lee House was used primarily as student housing. After the departure of the Phi Kappa Sigma fraternity in 2006, it became a residential option called "The Hub Theme Cottage," where technology-oriented students with a passion for computers, gaming, and "the core technologies of our society" can share living quarters, network, and offer programs and expertise to other SLU students.

You can be sure that with computers and other modern marvels of technology filling the ancient living quarters, residents will soon experience tampering of their equipment (if they haven't already). Unexplained computer issues are very common in haunted locations, like the nearby Kappa Delta Sigma house at 35 Park Street that I've written about in two previous books. But for now, the stories about the Lincoln Street ghost tell only of a female apparition seen "dashing around corners," wearing a long gown and a red petticoat. It reportedly despises rock-and-roll music and open doors, according to the former fraternity brothers interviewed for the SLU Sesquicentennial on the University's website. Lorraine Warren also sensed a female presence before coming face-to-face with it near a hallway radiator on the first floor. It was a middle-aged woman with hair tightly pulled back, wearing an apron over a plain, long dress. According to "Ghost Hunters at SLU Raise Friendly Spirit," an article written by Alison Power for the *Massena Observer* on January 16, 1979, Warren saw the spirit repeatedly placing an object in a cabinet in the butler's pantry. Ms. Power, who accompanied the Warrens and other students and journalists on the ghost hunt, said Mrs. Warren stressed that the house felt very peaceful and that the spirit she sensed was not a threat, by any means.

Could it be Elmina Bennett Lee, the lady of the house for forty-three years? She was known to love children. Perhaps she watches over the students who live in her former abode. Or maybe it's one of the Lee daughters—Leslie, Florence, or Gertrude—revisiting their childhood home. The 1870 Census of St. Lawrence County shows several other females living with the Lee family at 1 Lincoln Street at that time: Nora McCarter, a young domestic servant from Ireland; Martha Farwell, a middle-aged housekeeper; and Harriet Packard, the eleven-year-old daughter of an on-site wheelwright. The ghost lady of 1 Lincoln could be any one of them, whether they died there or not, simply returning to a place of familiarity.

Ghost of Mary Desmond

Burke

On September 4, 1906, George S. Henry, the Sheriff of Franklin County, offered a reward for a missing local woman: "I hereby offer a reward of $100 for information that will lead to the finding of the body of Mary Desmond, if dead, who disappeared from her home in Burke on August 20th, 1906, or that will establish her whereabouts if living." Mrs. Desmond's body was never found, dead or alive, but by 1910, four years after she disappeared, locals believed her spirit had returned to (or remained at) her former abode.

The house that Mrs. Desmond occupied with her son, Dennis, was located in the Sun area, about a mile north of Burke Center on the Coveytown Road. At about 10 P.M. on the evening of August 21, 1906, neighbors of the elderly woman were horrified to see that her house was consumed in flames. By the time they got to it, the interior was already engulfed, making it impossible to enter the building. All anyone could do was stand by and watch it burn, and hope that Mrs. Desmond and her son had escaped and gone for help. But when no one had seen either of them by the next morning, a grim search commenced for signs of their remains. Because the house and all that was in it had been virtually incinerated, all there was to sift through was a basement full of ashes. It was there, amid the knee-deep ashes, that a blackened object resembling a human skull was found. The *Adirondack News* of September 1, 1906, said, "The charred object found in the cellar, wrapped in a piece of cloth, around which were the [rosary] beads and cross, had the appearance of a human being."

When Mary Desmond's so-called skull was found but the rest of her

83

body was not, it was assumed she had been murdered and that her headless body was removed from the scene. But a local physician and a coroner, upon further examination of the skull-shaped object, determined the next day that it was, in fact, not a human skull. What it was, they didn't attempt to speculate. Nor did they explain how the rosary found with the object originally believed to be Mrs. Desmond's skull had survived a fire that incinerated everything but the skull-shaped object. Had Mary Desmond been a victim of Spontaneous Human Combustion, the bizarre, unexplainable phenomenon in which victims' bodies are rapidly incinerated, yet, for whatever the reason, random body parts and nearby furnishings are not only spared, but also left virtually unscathed? Had her skull become so altered in composition from the unusually hot fire, like the skulls of other victims of SHC, that it was impossible for the physicians to recognize it as such? The phenomenon would explain the lack of other body parts found in the ashes and the speed in which the fire consumed the house and its owner, if she was, in fact, inside. It would also help explain how some objects remained strangely unscathed, like the rosary beads and a money box also found in the ruins. Regardless of whether Mrs. Desmond was a victim of SHC or not, the findings of the physicians left the community scratching their heads.

When it was eventually discovered that Dennis, the woman's slight, 42-year-old son, did not die in the fire, he was initially suspected in her disappearance because he was considered to be "of unsound mind," having been in (and allegedly escaped from) a "lunatic asylum" at some point in his past. He and his mother had moved to Burke a few years earlier following the death of Mr. Desmond, who hanged himself at their home in the town of Constable. And now this. But Dennis had been away at the time of the fire, travelling by foot and rail to Valleyfield, Quebec, to purchase a new suit, and his alibi was confirmed. The *Chateaugay Record* said that Dennis's "grief over the death of his mother was genuine and pathetic," and his reaction convinced those who had formerly believed he was somehow involved to change their minds. Still, this was a man who admitted to his interrogators that a machine he called a "multiscope" governed his actions and was operated by his enemies. And, therefore, he said, "if he was told to kill his mother, he would not have the power to resist," according to the Chateaugay Record. But with no body, and apparently not even a skull, and with no clues or leads that panned out, there was no way to pin the blame on anyone, including Dennis Desmond. Nobody ever determined how Mrs. Desmond disappeared—if she perished in the flames that evening, or if, for whatever reason, she simply set the house afire and walked into the night with no intention of ever returning. For many years, it was the general opinion that she had been murdered and robbed and that the house had been set ablaze to hide the crime, but that theory, like all the others, has never been proven. Dennis was returned to the state hospital in Ogdensburg shortly after his mother's disappearance, and the property was put up for sale.

On March 3, 1910, the *Massena Observer* ran an article called "A Haunted House: Burke People See Spooks Where Woman Disappeared." The article stated that neighbors claimed the ruins of the Desmond house were haunted by "spooks" that occupied the cellar, making strange noises in the night. A door could be heard opening and slamming shut after midnight some nights, even though no door (or anything else, for that matter) remained. "No one is ever seen," the article said, "and they can't explain the mystery." As is often the case, from one unsolved mystery springs forth another.

Paddock Mansion

Watertown

The Paddock Mansion at 228 Washington Street has a rich and colorful history, making it the perfect location for its current occupant, the Jefferson County Historical Society… as well as the perfect venue for a few resident ghosts. The Historical Society doesn't deny that the property may be haunted. In fact, they included it in their 2008 Legends of Public Square walking tour that took participants to a number of well-known "spirited haunts," as they call them. The mansion was also the first stop on WPBS TV's 2008 Folklore & Frost bus tour that visited five of the area's most haunted locations. So what's all the hype about? First, a little history is in order.

The earliest framed house in the village of Watertown was built on the site of the Paddock Mansion in 1803 by Hart Massey. Five years later, Massey sold the house to Erastus Baker, who moved the house to Clinton Street, leaving a vacant lot at 228 Washington. He then sold the lot to a successful local storeowner and gristmill operator named Jabez Foster II, who would go on to become a president of the Jefferson County Bank and a judge for the Court of Common Pleas. In 1808, Foster built a grand Georgian mansion and other buildings on the site of the current Paddock Mansion and moved in with his wife, Hannah, and three children: Gustavus Adolphus, Elvira Lorraine, and Evalina. A second son, three-year-old Ambrose Sylvester, had died two years before their move to Watertown. While living at 228 Washington, Hannah and Jabez had eight more children: another Ambrose, Jabez, Hannah, Asa, Morris, Frederick, another Hannah (after the first died), and Harriet. Of those, six did not survive childhood, despite the best efforts of their

loving parents. This is important to note, considering some of the paranormal activity that currently occurs there.

To give you an idea of the early nineteenth-century life of the
Fosters, consider the following newspaper account of an event that took
place at the residence. It's from a column called "A Link in the Chain"
by Solon Massey in the *Daily New York Reformer* of August 7, 1863:

> Mrs. Foster was, notwithstanding, a woman of rare
> capacity and nerve on occasions of necessity or danger, as
> was demonstrated at a time somewhere about that period
> [1810], when one of her little girls fell into a deep well at the
> door, when the resolute mother, without any hesitation,
> climbed over the curb and down to the water, where she
> seized her child and, without any assistance, brought her out
> alive. It would have been a feat for any ordinary man, and her
> maternal instincts had seemed to serve her almost supernatu-
> rally for so difficult, not to say, dangerous, [a] task.

By all accounts, Hannah Hungerford Foster was a doting mother,
and the loss of seven of their twelve children must have been devastating.
She died young, at forty-nine years of age, in 1826, and her bereaved
husband found it too difficult to remain in the home where his wife and
so many of their children had died. Foster sold the mansion the same
year Hannah passed away and moved to Michigan to live with his wid-
owed daughter. There, he died of a heart attack in 1847.

In 1832, Loveland Paddock, a very wealthy financier and entrepre-
neur, purchased the Foster mansion and settled in with his wife, Sophia,
and three young sons—Oscar, George Foster, and Edwin—all of whom
lived to ripe old ages. It was Loveland Paddock who founded and
presided over the Black River Bank in 1844 and had the famous (and
equally haunted) Paddock Arcade built in 1850. Today, that arcade is
considered to be the oldest continuously-operating covered mall in the
nation. In 1872, Loveland and Sophia both died, he at the ripe age of
ninety-eight, and she at seventy-eight. Upon the illustrious couple's
passing, the estate went to their sons. Edwin bought out his brothers'

shares in the property and moved back into his childhood home with his wife, Olive. But the middle-aged couple sacrificed sentimentality for new construction and had the family home razed. In 1878, a new house was built in its place to their specifications—the three-story Paddock Mansion that we know and love today. Though the couple never had any children, their magnificent home and its gardens must have brought them much happiness, for they were obviously tended with great love and care. In 1896, Olive's mother passed away at the residence where she had been living with the couple. On July 22, 1909, Edwin Paddock also passed away there, at the age of eighty-five. As was customary at the time, the funeral was held in the home prior to his burial at Brookside Cemetery. The elderly Olive continued to live in the big old mansion alone, refusing to let her beloved home be razed for development, even as the mansions surrounding it disappeared and were replaced with various commercial and civic buildings. Determined to preserve the home she had put her stamp on for more than four decades, Olive bequeathed the Paddock Mansion to the Jefferson County Historical Society upon her death in 1922. Many people believe she still lingers…as hesitant to give up her home in death as she was in life.

In 1924, after the requisite renovations for a public facility were made, the mansion opened as a museum, and in 1979, it was listed on the National Register of Historic Places. Today, Paddock Mansion (both inside and out) is eye candy for aficionados of old homes and historic buildings. Because Edwin wanted a Victorian home and Olive preferred a Swiss chalet, the architect designed it as a stunning combination of both. The public is encouraged to roam through the grounds, three floors of the mansion (the basement, first, and second), a Victorian garden, and three outbuildings. Period furnishings adorn the parlor, and the remaining rooms include collections and exhibits of local and Paddock family history. The life-size (and greater-than-life-size) Tuthill portraits are at once impressive and unnerving, with eyes that seem to follow you, as those in portraits sometimes do. Fittingly, there was a "Victorian Macabre" exhibit the last few times I visited that displayed mourning costumes and funeral attire of the Victorian era, as well as post-mortem photographs and jewelry crafted of the hair of the deceased—a custom common in the Victorian age. In a building widely believed to be haunted, such an exhibit is certainly appropriate.

According to the walking tour script for the Legends of Public Square tour, many people believe it is Olive's spirit that primarily haunts the home since she was so attached to it in life. Lights come on in the unoccupied museum at night, and the subtle sound of doors closing, footsteps, and mysterious chattering are often heard by individuals working alone in the building. In 2008, a person walking past the museum late one night adamantly claims to have seen the figure of a woman whose outline was eerily backlit looking out the windows of the front door. When the shocked observer stopped to take a second glance, the figure turned and walked into the next room before disappearing. She was dressed in Victorian garb. A similarly-dressed young woman was seen walking through the garden by a former employee. It took the employee only a few seconds to reach the back door to investigate, but the woman had disappeared. Although many staff members and visitors believe it to be Olive's spirit, I think it may be that of Hannah Foster, the doting mother who, along with six of her children, died prematurely on those very grounds—albeit in a house that was razed to make way for the current Mansion. Hannah's spirit would appear younger, as witnesses have said the apparition did. She was only forty-nine when she died, whereas Olive was in her late eighties. And Olive's mother, who also passed away in the home, was eighty-three at the time of her death, so Hannah seems the most likely match to the apparition people have seen.

That said, there have been other incidents that I think perhaps Olive is more likely to be responsible for. A former curator had searched in vain in the storage area on the third floor for items belonging to a specific collection being readied for display. Giving up, she returned to work the next day and found the items she needed sitting right on her desk. Every single staff member was grilled to determine who had put them there, but nobody had. This is a common phenomenon in haunted places: objects disappear and then reappear some time later in a very obvious location. The reason Olive would be the most likely culprit for this particular stunt is that she was most familiar with the current building and would know where items—especially those connected to her family—

were located. It's possible she has been watching over the museum for years, taking note of where her earthly possessions have been placed.

Psychics visiting the mansion have sensed a number of spirits, including a Civil War soldier who stood in the second-floor hallway, glanced over at the psychic, and walked calmly into the room housing the Civil War exhibit, disappearing there without a trace. The kitchen in the basement has a crib in which a child is believed to have died, and its spirit is thought to be the lone orb that frequently appears in photographs taken in that room. My own photograph (below) showed an obvious orb next to the nearby sink, and a number of people taking photographs on the PBS bus tour were thrilled to see that they, too, had captured an orb hovering over the crib. If that isn't enough, the Shadow Chasers of Potsdam recorded an EVP of a baby crying during their investigation of the site in 2008, and they also filmed an "energy anomaly" near the crib. Now, I'm not sure whose family the crib belonged to, but I do know that the Fosters lost seven of their twelve children on those very grounds, most as babies or toddlers. Their children were the only ones known to have died as youngsters on that property, so I believe one of the Foster

Photo by author.

Basement kitchen in Paddock Mansion, with orb hovering near sink.

91

children is the baby heard crying and the spirit seen hovering over the crib. The only other explanation would be that the crib came from an entirely different property, and the little soul is attached to the crib, rather than the property itself.

The Shadow Chasers set up a remote camera in the upstairs hallway of the mansion and then left the building to let it record. When they returned, they said, "the camera had been shifted, and all of the footage filmed was grainy." There are any number of spirits that might be blamed for activities such as objects (including the Shadow Chasers' equipment) moving, doors heard opening and closing, the chattering that seems to have no source, and the footsteps: Loveland, Sophia, Edwin, Olive, Olive's mother, Hannah and her children, or even her husband, Jabez, who perhaps returns to the property longing for the wife and children he lost there, even though the home he shared with them has long since been replaced.

BrightSide on Raquette

Raquette Lake

A tragic love story. A mysterious disappearance. An ill-timed blizzard. A remote Adirondack luxury resort accessible only by boat. These are the ingredients of a timeless tale of ghosts served up at the BrightSide on Raquette located at Indian Point on Raquette Lake.

Joe and Mary Bryere were the quintessential hard-working, tireless North Country settlers when they began construction of their dream resort in the 1880s. By the time that dream had been realized, the BrightSide was a hundred-acre vacation complex with a hotel (the structure this story is about), cabins, a water tower, and a boathouse that offered activities such as water sports, golf, and tennis. It became a popular Adirondack resort that catered, in its heyday, to the wealthy. Joe Bryere continued to run the business until his death in 1941. At that time, one of the couple's four grown children, Clara, took over and soon became known as "Miss BrightSide" because of her capable manner of running the place and the much-needed improvements she implemented. She maintained the family business until 1957, when she sold the inn to BrightSide on Raquette Lake Incorporated. Then, in 2001, the Light Connection, a telecommunications firm owned by Frank Grotto, purchased the property and brought it up to code with structural repairs and a complete overhaul of the plumbing and heating. The company now uses the site as a corporate training facility for Mr. Grotto's three companies, but they also offer it to other groups and individuals for special events, company retreats, training seminars, and such.

The owners are not at all bashful regarding ghost stories associated with BrightSide. Their official website includes an entire page detailing many of the incidents believed to be paranormal in nature that they and others have experienced. In fact, there is one room over the kitchen that they call the Ghost Room, and a running list of ghostly happenings at BrightSide is posted just outside of that room. *Why, you ask?* Because of an incident that took place over a hundred years ago. In the midst of a blinding snowstorm, a couple checked into the inn, but before getting too comfortable, the man set out for the village for supplies. Nobody knows what he was thinking when he crossed the frozen lake in zero visibility; what is known is that he never returned. His tracks were covered in snow practically as soon as he made them. There was no trace of the missing man, and it was assumed he got lost and perished in the blizzard. It is said that his heartbroken wife kept vigil at the window of the couple's guest room (the one now dubbed the Ghost Room) and never stopped waiting for her husband to return...even after she died.

When the Light Connection's renovators commenced work, they found a woman's Victorian-era coat hanging on a coat rack in that room. It was in perfect shape, especially considering its obvious age, and to this day, nobody knows why or by whom it was left there. At the time, none of the workers were aware of the story about the ill-fated couple connected to that room. Several months later, a Victorian-era gentleman's coat was discovered hanging beside the woman's coat on the same coat rack. BrightSide's website says that nobody knows "where, when, or how it got there." A young girl who was unaware of the stories was assigned that guest room one night several years ago. She was alarmed when her bed began to shake so violently that she could barely hold onto the book she was reading. Another woman staying in the room on a different occasion thought she heard her camera taking pictures one morning as she made the bed. She thought nothing more of it until several weeks later when she had the film from her BrightSide visit developed. Three photographs *had* been taken from the spot where the camera was resting when she heard it clicking that morning. Incredibly, each of those photographs showed blue orbs. I've heard a lot of things in this business, but a ghost photographing another ghost? That's a first.

Blue orbs were also seen by a male guest one night. He told his traveling companions and the staff that he had been transfixed by the way the lights from boats on the lake reflected off his windows, causing blue spheres to appear to dance around his room. He seemed almost giddy recalling the light show until he was snapped back to reality with a teasing reminder that his room didn't *face* the lake…and that the blue orbs were likely a spirit manifestation. The poor guy was one of the first in his party to check out. In August 2002, the Mohawk Valley Ghost Hunters investigated the resort's grounds and captured blue orbs on film. According to BrightSide's Web site, a copy of their investigative report stating that the original building is indeed "very active" is kept on site for all guests to enjoy.

Drake Mountain

Keeseville

I love old newspapers, with their curious headlines and whimsical, catchy subtitles. I could read them all day. While searching for long-forgotten ghost stories in online newspaper archives, I came across an interesting article in the *Essex County Republican* of July 23, 1915. The first title that caught my eye on the page in question was "Aged Keeseville Woman Claimed by Grim Reaper." Can you imagine today's newspapers using such a depressing title for an obituary? As appropriate as that title sounded for what I write about, the story wasn't the one I was looking for. The article I sought was in the next column over, titled: "Terrible Story of Mystery and Adventure is Related—Fearless Joe, Handsome Harry, Eagle Eye Charlie, and Camping Jerry Spend Night in Haunted House." *Now* we're talking.

It all began one summer day in 1915 with an argument between old friends over—of all things—who could pick the most blueberries. (Talk about simple times!) Fearless Joe challenged the other three to a berry-picking contest on Drake Mountain in Port Douglass, near Keeseville, Essex County. The pine-oak forest of Drake Mountain is known for its gorgeous views of Lake Champlain and its bountiful natural resources, including, apparently, blueberries. So the village quartet, as they were fondly called, set out one unforgettable Sunday for a vacant hunting shack they knew about that had "long been noted for its spooks and ghosts," according to the article. It would serve as their campsite for the night, and they would get up early the next morning, after a good night's sleep, to begin their friendly competition. That was the plan, at least, and they had hoped to stick to it. After all, Fearless Joe had a reputation to uphold as the area's champion berry picker.

The men arrived at their destination on schedule and retired at dusk, falling easily asleep in the blissful silence of the remote campsite. About an hour later, the silence was interrupted by what they later described as a "slight rapping" on the roof. Fearless Joe was first to hear it. As the sound became steadier and more pronounced, Joe roused the others, and the four big, brave men sat bug-eyed in the darkness, chills running up their spines, contemplating what their next move should be.

"Get the axe," shouted Fearless Joe, in a trembling voice. "*You* get it!" yelled Handsome Harry. The foursome debated thusly, but nobody dared move. "We don't need the axe," said Camping Jerry. "Let's get out of here!" But the men only made it as far as the barn, where they had left their horse. Once they saw that the horse was okay, they headed back into the shack. After all, if the horse wasn't spooked, why should they be? Horses have keen instincts—some even call it a sixth sense. It must've been nothing or their horse would have been dancing around in a frightened state, not standing calmly with its eyes half closed as they found it. The men, feeling assured, returned to their slumber.

According to the article:

> A few minutes passed, and then without warning, down came the curtain from the window. White, flickering, ghostly shadows passed to and thro'. The rapping continued and weird shrieks rent the air. By this time, it was three o'clock in the morning, and the berry pickers had no further intention of sleeping.

Instead, they ate a hardy breakfast and waited for the sun to rise so they could accomplish what they had set out to do. Bidding the little shack of horrors adieu, they set out to pick their berries. After several hours, they headed home, stopping at Port Douglass along their route. All but Fearless Joe disembarked from the wagon. The horse was contentedly chewing on a blade of grass, with Joe lightly holding the reigns, when suddenly, it became spooked for no apparent reason, with no warning. Joe was forced to tighten his grip and hold on for dear life, or he'd surely be thrown. After much commotion, the animal was brought under control, and the men continued home with some colorful tales to tell. Had the spook of Drake Mountain bummed a ride with the men into Port Douglass? Had the horse experienced a delayed reaction to the events that had transpired the previous evening? And, perhaps most importantly of all, did Fearless Joe manage to defend his berry-picking title?

Quiet Lady

Fort Drum

When Christina[*] and Michael[*] were in the process of moving from the notoriously-haunted Fort Leavenworth Army post in Kansas to their new digs at Fort Drum, they were given a standard housing check-out form to fill out. All outgoing tenants are asked to provide information regarding any problems they experienced in the housing unit they occupied so that future tenants will know what to expect (or so that the problem can be rectified prior to the next occupant's arrival). Christina said a typical comment you might list would be "toilet tends to run and run" or "windows are drafty"—that sort of thing. Imagine her surprise when she and Michael got to the part on the government-issued form asking specifically about paranormal experiences! She said, "To me, this was the U.S. Government acknowledging the existence of ghosts and/or spirits on post…I thought it was pretty profound that we were asked to document any [such] experiences." Thankfully, they hadn't had any while living at that base, but their Fort Drum housing experience is another story.

The couple lives in a community of new construction and renovated homes for officers' families on South Fort Drum (toward the Black River end). Their house is new and was built on a concrete slab, like hundreds of others in that area. Christina searched through photo archives of Fort Drum and I searched through old newspaper archives, both of us trying to find out what was on the land before the housing units dotted the landscape, but we came up empty-handed. Still, with a full-blown apparition clearly witnessed by two and heard by one, there can be no doubt that the house is haunted. Christina told me that right from the start, she felt as if she wasn't alone in the house, but she didn't tell anyone or dwell on it because it didn't upset her; she assumed she was the only one who noticed it. She stressed that this is not a story about a frightening ghost or a terrible experience, insisting, "Our spirit is friendly, discreet, non-invasive, and seems to be passing through now and then. We are absolutely not afraid of her. She does not make the hair stand up on the back of necks, and she is not mischievous in any way."

The "Quiet Lady" made her presence known very delicately at first. Christina simply saw "dark, gray, shadowy spots the size of a dish towel flash through the air and disappear into the ceiling" and chalked it up to eye floaters (physiological spots in one's visual field). And sometimes in the kitchen, she would turn around and catch a glimpse of "a shadowy substance" quickly disappearing, as if it had been watching her work and scrambled to hide when she turned around. But she reasoned that her tired eyes must be seeing things. Then, one day, as her daughter's friend was standing nearby petting their dog, Christina suddenly saw something indistinct flash past her toward the window that looks out over the backyard. At virtually the same moment, she heard something that sounded like a pebble hit the glass on that same window. Her daughter's friend hadn't heard it, though, so Christina figured it must have been something outside. Just then, it happened again, and this time they both heard it. The two searched in vain for the object that caused the sound but found nothing. The Quiet Lady was coming out of her shell…

As it turned out, Michael would be the first to see the full-blown apparition of their coy spectral visitor. He had just returned from a deployment and was relaxing in front of the television with Christina, who had turned to face him. As he looked at her, Michael had a clear view of the kitchen behind her. The two were discussing dinner plans when she noticed him looking over her shoulder. He then blurted out, "Wow, that is so wild!" When Christina asked what was so wild about her dinner idea, Michael said, "No, the woman standing behind you is wild. There was a ghost standing behind you just now." Michael had never been much of a believer in ghosts, so the fact that he was the first to see the spirit was significant to Christina, even if she was a bit envious. He described the apparition as "definitely female"…and definitely white, transparent, and faceless. He said it stood behind Christina only for a moment, then disappeared into the kitchen.

One night some time later, Christina had an even closer encounter. She was asleep on the couch when the sound of her dogs walking toward the back door (to go out) awakened her. She opened her eyes and looked toward the hallway, expecting to see them, and that was when she saw *her* instead—their Quiet Lady. The apparition was "floating in the center of the hallway, just very gently and peacefully," she said. Too tired to care, Christina closed her eyes and attempted to go back to sleep. About ten minutes passed before she opened her eyes again. This time, she watched, mesmerized; the silent apparition was much closer now, between Christina and the coffee table in front of the sofa, moving, Christina reported "as if she was just passing through that space to get somewhere else." And then she was gone.

The couple's teenage daughter hasn't had a visual encounter yet, but she had a very memorable auditory (and physical) sensation. She was standing quietly one day, looking out the window into the front yard, when she heard someone whisper clearly, but gently, into her ear, "Hi." At the same time, she felt someone's breath on her ear, as if that someone was actually standing right there, that close to her. It was her only encounter with the resident ghost, and, like her parents' encounters, it was benign. The entire family agrees that whoever this Quiet Lady is, at least she's friendly and gentle. But Christina does wonder if there's "more than just her, because [the Quiet Lady] is so light and white, yet the shadows are grayish."

The family will be moving to Fort Riley in northern Kansas this summer, and Christina has mixed feelings about leaving the spirit she's become accustomed to (even though she's been told Fort Riley has plenty of ghosts to go around). "I actually feel bad leaving her," she said of their quiet Fort Drum ghost. Then she added mischievously, "I feel bad that the incoming family will find out about her the hard way." Her primary reason for sharing her story with me was to have it documented, because, she said, "I sincerely doubt Housing will pass along our experiences to the next occupants of our home, especially since it is brand new housing. And one day, someone might start to wonder about this place." Even though this story is anonymous, it should help other military families at Fort Drum realize they are not alone if they find themselves living in a haunted house. In fact, Christina recently spoke with someone else in the neighborhood who acknowledged that they, too, were having strange experiences, though the person hesitated to elaborate.

Obviously, if the government is willing to put information about ghosts on paper at Fort Leavenworth, haunted military bases must be fairly common. And we *know* Fort Drum is. I've already written stories about its haunted Sheepfold (Prisoner-of-War) Cemetery, as well as the LeRay Mansion. This story is just one more drop in the bucket.

St. Lawrence River Ghost-Witch

Waddington

Our Canadian neighbors have long told a legend of an Iroquois Indian witch named Matshi Skoueow. During the eighteenth century, her reviled spirit roamed up and down the St. Lawrence River between Waddington on the United States side and Iroquois Point on Canadian shores, looking for victims for the Iroquois to torture.

J. Castell Hopkins, in his 1913 work, *French Canada and the St. Lawrence*, mentions the "weird and melancholy" tale from Abbe H.R. Casgrain's *Canadian Legends*. According to Hopkins, a man named LeCanotier left Quebec one day around 1713 with his Indian paddler and a beautiful, well-dressed young woman and her nine-year-old son. The woman, Madam Houel, had hired LeCanotier to take her to her husband, whom she learned had "suffered a serious accident." At the time, traveling by boat was a dangerous undertaking, as the Iroquois were a force to be reckoned with on the St. Lawrence River. Any and all who traveled the waters near Iroquois Point were at risk of being captured by Iroquois Indians seeking vengeance for the defeat and slaughter of a hundred brothers at that spot not many years earlier.

LeCanotier was well aware of the risk when he accepted the job. He was also well aware of the possibility of seeing the legendary witch of the St. Lawrence who seemed to serve the Iroquois. As the canoe made its way silently down the river under the cover of darkness, the sleeping boy suddenly awoke, frightened, saying there was a woman in white walking on the water. The others were unable to see the apparition, but LeCanotier knew that children were more open to seeing ghosts than adults. His worst fear was about to become a reality, as he realized that the boy's vision was Matshi Skoueow and they had invaded not only her territory, but also the Iroquois territory she guarded. He knew that sightings of the apparition always preceded capture by the Iroquois. Almost immediately, the Iroquois were upon them, and in the scuffle, the beautiful madam was slaughtered, LeCanotier and the paddler escaped, and the boy was taken captive. Years later, the guilt-ridden LeCanotier returned to rescue Madam Houel's son. For many years following that incident, children on both sides of the river were warned against going near the shore for fear that the witch of the St. Lawrence was awaiting her next innocent victim.

Today, the Iroquois Dam spans nearly 2,000 feet across the St. Lawrence River from Waddington to Iroquois Point, the spot where many lives were brutally cut short. So, if you see a lady in white, or a single, white orb, or if you hear a haunting melody out on the river but can find no source for it, it may be the tragic spirit of Madam Houel. Pray for her soul. But if, instead, it's the blood-thirsty St. Lawrence River Ghost-Witch, pray for your own.

Haunted Motel

Massena

Bud* began our conversation by stressing that he was just a typical Army sergeant with a pretty level head and a logical explanation for everything. However, because of the nature of this book and the fact that he's still in the military, he requested that I not reveal his name or that of the motel he was staying at when this story took place, although I do know the identity of both. This is Bud's story.

In November 2001, shortly after (and as a result of) the September 11 terrorist attacks, Bud and his comrades were working closely with Customs and Border Protection (CBP), touring ports of entry throughout the state. They had been on the road for about a month by the time they reached Massena, which was to be their last stop before returning to the base in Buffalo where they were stationed. Somehow, their original motel reservations got mixed up, and they found themselves without rooms and looking for another place to stay. The group eventually checked into a local motel that was built on land cleared in the early 1800s.

Nothing it its history can explain the experience Bud and his companions had during their unplanned stay at the motel. However, many people pass through the doors of lodging establishments, and, in this case, they had been doing so for fifty years. Motels, hotels, hospitals, theaters, and schools are known to be among the most haunted structures, not necessarily because there have been deaths on site, but because so many people have passed through. Even if someone didn't die at a location that is now haunted, the person may have spent much time there, or stayed only briefly, but at a pivotal point in his or her life. Such scenarios result in hauntings as often as cases where an individual actually died at a place. I found nothing to indicate any tragedies, crimes, or deaths had ever occurred at this particular motel prior to Bud's experience. And yet…and yet, something so alarming allegedly happened to the four parties involved that they made a hasty retreat after just one night's occupancy.

Shortly after Mark*, Mary*, and Bud had settled into their respective adjacent rooms, Mary went to Bud's room to complain about the noisy party apparently happening directly over her room. Then Mark showed up with the same complaint. His and Mary's rooms were on either side of Bud's, yet there was no sound of partying over Bud's room (nor had there been since he arrived). The trio was too tired and hungry to give it any more thought at the time. But it would certainly leave them scratching their heads a bit later.

They decided to hang out in Bud's quiet room for dinner. While the two men went to pick up some beverages, Mary stayed behind to wait for the pizza delivery. Climbing into the van, Bud happened to look back at the motel and noticed something surprising: *There was no floor above them!* They were already on the top floor, so there couldn't have been a party overhead. *What the…?* He and Mark couldn't believe it.

When they returned to the motel several minutes later, their timing seemed perfect. Mary was standing outside of Bud's door next to the pizza guy, though she must have changed clothes while they were away because she was wearing a different outfit. As Mark and Bud proceeded toward the building, they passed the delivery man and nodded in acknowledgment. But when they walked through the door to Bud's room, Mary was wearing her original clothing…and there was no pizza in sight! She had no idea what they were talking about when they asked her what happened to her clothes, let alone the pizza they saw delivered to their room. This was getting weirder by the moment.

Determined to find out what was going on, Bud called the front desk. "I'm not trying to sound weird or anything," he told the front desk clerk, "but has anyone ever reported anything strange going on at this motel?" The response was a curt, "No." *Click.* Alrighty, then…that went well. They were beginning to feel like pawns trapped in the *Twilight Zone*.

Thankfully, the rest of their night was uneventful, but early the next morning, their lieutenant, whose room was not far from theirs in the same motel, roused them out of their slumber and told them to pack up. They were moving to another motel now. From the urgency in her voice, and the fact that she wouldn't say why they had to leave so quickly, they could only assume that she, too, had experienced something she couldn't explain. So, if you're ever staying at a motel in Massena and you experience something you believe to be paranormal in nature, know that you're not alone.

Ghost of Pulpit Rock

Lake Placid

Drowning is not so pitiful
As the attempt to rise
Three times, 'tis said, a sinking man
Comes up to face the skies,
And then declines forever
To that abhorred abode
Where hope and he part company,
For he is grasped of God…

Emily Dickinson

A ghost would have to be pretty important to have a popular cocktail named after it. Mabel Smith Douglass is Lake Placid's own VIP specter, and the posh Hilton Lake Placid Resort named its signature drink, the "Lady in the Lake," after her. Served on the resort's seasonal cocktail cruise, the ingredients of the beverage—the name of which was made famous by Chris Ortloff's book of the same name (concerning the same incident)—include cranberry juice, ginger ale, vodka, and lime…topped with a tragic tale of death and resurrection, sort of. The story—and sightings of the apparition believed to be that of Smith Douglass—began after her mysterious disappearance on September 21, 1933, when her overturned rowboat was found drifting, empty, near Pulpit Rock.

Born Anna Mabel Smith in Jersey City in 1877, Smith Douglass earned her bachelor's degree from Barnard College in 1899, becoming one of the first graduates of that school. She then taught elementary school in New York City until her marriage to William Douglass in 1903. A son and a daughter were born to the couple, and life was good. But Smith Douglass had a burning desire to do more for women and education. In 1911, while the children were still quite young, she decided that the all-male Rutgers College needed a sister counterpart. Using her own money, along with funds she raised through tremendous hard work and diligence, that dream would become a reality within seven years, but another dream—the dream of a happy home—had already perished, and it had taken a toll on Smith Douglass's health. By the time the New Jersey College for Women (now known as Douglass College) opened in 1918 with Smith Douglass as its first dean, her beloved husband and mother had both passed away. More tragedy would soon follow, further tempering the smallest shred of happiness she could muster. In 1923, Smith Douglass's son, not yet a man, committed suicide, yet the devastated dean somehow pressed on until May 1933, when, with her own health deteriorating and her heart just not in it anymore, Mabel Smith Douglass resigned her position as dean and moved to her family's camp near the Whiteface Inn on the shores of Lake Placid. There, on September 21, 1933, just four months after bidding adieux to the college she founded, she vanished near Pulpit Rock, where she was last seen alive, alone in a St. Lawrence skiff rowboat. The boat was found capsized, and a massive search was undertaken, but no body was found to put closure to the case, that is, not until September 15, 1963—one week short of the thirty-year anniversary of her disappearance.

Frank Pabst was starting his own scuba diving company and had just purchased the "Sea Witch," a thirty-two-foot excursion boat, when he came upon a gruesome discovery while attempting to explore the submerged cliffs of Pulpit Rock that September day. At first, he and the other diver believed they were looking at a discarded store mannequin; however, on closer inspection, they could tell it was a human body. The water temperature where the body was found some 105 feet below the surface was near freezing, at thirty-four degrees Fahrenheit. The individual they were looking at had been remarkably well-preserved in a substance called adipocere, more commonly known as grave wax. When a corpse is exposed to certain conditions—primarily high moisture, low oxygen, and lack of microorganisms and wildlife that would feed on it—adipocere naturally forms over the body as a normal part of decomposition. This condition is not uncommon in drowning victims, but that didn't make it any less startling to the poor divers who happened upon the remains.

They discovered the body lying on its right side on a blanket of silt with a rope knotted around its neck. The other end of the rope was connected to an anchor, but when they touched the rope it disintegrated, sending the anchor deeper into the silt and the corpse toward the surface. The divers followed, gently guiding their gruesome find to the surface, where they secured it to a buoy and prepared to lift it onto the boat. In that short period of time, while they were scrambling to lift the cadaver as carefully as they could, several speed boats zoomed by, causing waves to jostle the buoy. The sudden jarring of the delicate remains caused the corpse to crumble right before the eyes of the horrified divers. The head, neck, left arm, and right hand all fell off and sank below the surface. Although another diver was quickly sent down to retrieve the fallen body parts, they had already settled into four feet of silt, making it virtually impossible. The determined diver did, however, find the head—but it was in a far worse shape now than it had been moments earlier. When the corpse was first discovered, the facial features were quite recognizable—and they were etched into the memories of the two original divers—but the features quickly disintegrated when the remains were jostled about. The divers didn't know who the victim was, and they had never heard about the disappearance of Mabel Smith Douglass, but the locals clued them in, as well as the troopers investigating their discovery.

After an exhaustive investigation, including findings from the autopsy and examination of the teeth, it was determined that the body was, in fact, that of the long-missing dean of Douglass College. There was eventually enough evidence for the Bureau of Criminal Investigation in Saranac Lake to issue a statement saying that "the official coroner's verdict is accidental death," even though many believe it was a suicide, for there was plenty of evidence to support that theory.

Smith Douglass's remains were claimed by Douglass College and buried at the Greenwood Cemetery in Brooklyn next to the graves of her husband and children. Her daughter, for a time the only surviving family member, died from a tragic fall fifteen years after her mother disappeared, never knowing what had become of her.

A number of people over the years have seen a misty, white apparition wafting eerily in the air near Pulpit Rock and assumed it must be Mabel's spirit, still bound to the place where she died. But if Pulpit Rock is haunted, there have been others who met untimely deaths there that may also share the blame. The *Adirondack Record-Elizabethtown Post*, dated November 1, 1923, ten years before Smith Douglass drowned, reported:

> An overturned canoe, floating on Lake Placid near Pulpit Rock, told the grim story of a mountain climbing expedition in which two men lost their lives. Ten minutes later, searchers found the body of Raymond Osborne, a carpenter employed at the Lake Placid Club, in seven feet of water. The search was continued later in the hope of finding the body of Patrick Greeley, Osborne's companion.

The last article regarding the double drowning ran in the *Lake Placid News* on November 2, 1923, in a story called, "Still Searching for Body of Pat Greeley." It says:

> Continued search was made for the body of Patrick Greeley on Friday and Saturday of last week and daily thru the week…It is believed by many familiar with the lake that the body will not rise naturally, due to the extremely low temperature of the water, and that the prospect of recovering the body…is slight.

So the body of Smith Douglass did not rest in the depths alone all those years. It joined that of Greeley, whose remains lie down there still, somewhere below Pulpit Rock.

Holcroft House

Potdsam

Clarkson University's Office of Admission and Welcome Center are located in Holcroft House, directly on the left as you enter campus via the main entrance from Maple Street (Route 11). The Clarkson family built the three-story, white house and founded the university, so it's only appropriate that family memorabilia be showcased in the Welcome Center, located in the former dining and living areas, where students and visitors can learn all about the family's contributions to the University and to the community…and perhaps catch a fleeting glimpse of the famous "Ghost of Holcroft." Potsdam Town Historian Betsy Baker told me that Holcroft immediately came to mind when I asked her about local haunted houses. She said, "I've spoken to people over the years who say they have heard footsteps in Holcroft House, lights that were turned off being on, doors that were closed being open, etc." Given that the house is fast approaching two hundred years of age, the idea that it may be haunted certainly isn't surprising.

In 1802, several male members of the Clarkson family jointly purchased a tract of land in Potsdam that was eight by ten miles large (just two miles short of the original ten by ten miles allocated to the town). Sixteen years later, the first member of the family, John Charlton Clarkson, arrived in Potsdam to take charge of the property. He built Holcroft House (or The Mansion, as it was called then) in 1822 and lived there until 1835, when he returned to New York City. Five years later, Levinus Clarkson arrived in town and moved into Holcroft, dying there in 1845. In 1852 or 1853, T. Streatfield Clarkson and his wife, Ann-Mary, moved into Holcroft, where they raised two daughters,

Annie and Emile, and lived the rest of their lives.

Annie Clarkson, who inherited the home when her father died in 1902, one hundred years after the family purchased the land, was the last Clarkson to ever use Holcroft as a private residence. Sometime later she moved to New York City, returning only during the summer months.

The *Potsdam Herald Recorder*, on December 10, 1926, said that only two of the Clarkson descendants remained living (Emile and Annie), and they lived elsewhere. "Aside from a few weeks in summer," the article said, "the residences [including Holcroft] in Potsdam stand vacant; and…it is unlikely they will be tenanted again." But the article was wrong: The following year, "Miss Annie" gave Clarkson University the entire Clarkson family estate, consisting of six hundred acres, as well as Holcroft, her beloved family home. She died in New York City in 1929.

Holcroft was used as an all-male dormitory for Clarkson students from the 1940s to the 1950s and as a women's dormitory in the 1960s and 1970s. It was during this latter time period that stories about "the ghost of Holcroft" first surfaced. The *Clarkson Integrator*, the university's official newspaper, has run countless articles about the alleged ghost, and the *Watertown Daily Times* ran a story in 1987 about a graduate who had a personal encounter with an apparition in her room one night in the early '70s. She looked up to see a young woman standing at the foot of her bed and looking at her, and she was surprised to find that the other residents of the house took it so lightly, apparently because ghost sightings and paranormal activity had become so common that they were all used to it by then. The apparition, as described by the many who had seen it, was a young woman (in her late twenties) wearing a long dark skirt or dress and a blouse with sleeves that were puffy on the upper arm and buttoned snuggly down the forearm. She had dark hair pulled off her face and, while lovely, she invariably appeared sad or tired. Dubbed "Elizabeth," a name gleaned from a Ouija board, she is believed to mostly haunt the third floor of Holcroft, where most of the activity seems to occur even now. Elizabeth is thought to perhaps be a servant because of her sad, tired appearance and because the servants' quarters were often on the third floor in those days. Census records do indicate that the wealthy Clarkson family employed help, as most prominent families did at the time. However, I didn't find records of any servant named Elizabeth. There was, however, the elderly Elizabeth Clarkson who, per census data, may have lived there with her daughter Ann-Mary (Annie Clarkson's mother) for a time in the 1870s. So, perhaps the mother of the university's namesake is the spirit of Holcroft, which would certainly be appropriate. What mother wouldn't want to welcome people to a college named after her child?

While few reports of actual apparitions have made the news in recent years, there are still accounts of possible paranormal activity coming out of Holcroft. Curtains open on their own, office equipment like the copier and calculators operate unassisted, furniture gets mysteriously moved around overnight, lights turn on and off, footsteps and banging have been heard…the usual ghostly phenomena. In 1999, the door to the third floor, which was always unlocked, was discovered inexplicably locked one day, according to the *Integrator* (October 25, 1999). Not a big deal in and of itself, by any means, but taken with the other incidents occurring at the time, it does make one wonder. In the same time frame, bookends once moved off the edge of a bookshelf as a mother and son who was being interviewed in Admissions watched in astonishment. Painters, according to the *Integrator* article, refused to work at night in the mid-nineties, after a number of unexplainable things happened while they were painting the health center, which was then housed in Holcroft. They claimed that just as they walked away after cleaning their brushes in the sink, the faucet would turn back on. What's more, their vehicles sometimes wouldn't start when they attempted to leave, and lights often flickered as they worked.

Stacey Tarbox is very familiar with the stories of Holcroft, because her father was a night security guard there for many years, and Stacey and her sisters sometimes went to work with him in the summertime. She said they always jumped at the opportunity to go, because they were curious to see if anything (ghostly) would happen. "We were never disappointed," she said, adding that she had seen shadows of people that weren't there and heard the door slam shut on the third floor, the same location where people have seen a woman in the window and heard a woman crying. Stacey said that for a while after her father retired in 1985, nobody wanted to work in offices on the third floor "because of all the unexplained noises and movements" up there.

So, *is* Holcroft House as haunted as many eyewitnesses believe it is? Staff aren't afraid to say so, even if Clarkson officials haven't admitted it. According to the aforementioned 1987 *Times* article, University officials at that time said "spirits have no place" in an institution of higher education that specializes in "science, engineering, and management." *Really?* Today's paranormal investigators, armed with enough technical gadgetry and scientific expertise to make a physics major drool, would certainly beg to differ.

Slaughter Hill

Brownville

> Vampire: A blood-sucking ghost; a soul of a dead person
> superstitiously believed to come from the grave and wander
> about by night sucking the blood of persons asleep...The per-
> sons who turn [into] vampires are generally wizards, witches,
> suicides, and persons who have come to a violent end...
> —*Webster's Revised Unabridged Dictionary* (1998)

In the summer of 1828, residents living on the outskirts of the village of Brownville became gripped by fear and panic in the wake of
multiple reports of vampire sightings. Superstition was alive and well in
the early nineteenth century, which is not to say that there's no such
thing as blood-sucking, life-zapping vampires—a subject out of my
realm of expertise—but I'm merely suggesting that perhaps it was
nothing more than a harmless ghost. Whatever it was, the residents
remedied the situation by moving the corpse they believed was rising
nightly from the dead to an unmarked grave in the middle of nowhere,
miles from town, where they hoped it might become someone else's
problem. The "corpse-on-wheels" was that of condemned murderer
Henry Evans.

"Evans lived on a piece of land owned by LeRay and leased to
Wilbur Rogers, who desired to dispossess Evans," according to an article
in the *Watertown Herald* dated November 10, 1900. The property was
on the Perch River Road (County Route 54) halfway between the town
of Brownville and the hamlet of Perch River. The Rogers family was in

disagreement over the matter of kicking Evans out. Wilbur's mother and his brother Benjamin pleaded with him to let Evans, a husband and father of two, remain in the house. But Wilbur and his other brother, Joshua, could not be swayed. The two, along with their friend and coworker Henry Dimond, stopped at Evans' house on their way home from work on April 16, drunk, and not in the mood to bargain. Evans had locked the door, but that didn't stop the hell-bent trio from getting in. Once inside, a heated argument ensued between Wilbur Rogers and Evans, with each demanding that the other get out. As the men closed in on him, Evans reached beneath the bed in desperation, and the next thing anyone knew, he was wielding an axe, and two men ended up slaughtered on the spot. As Evans was dragged off in handcuffs, the bodies of the two men lay on the property, but Wilbur, the mastermind of the failed operation, lived to tell about it.

Benjamin Rogers would later tell a jury that, on the night before the crime, he had heard his brother Wilbur say that he was going to take Joshua and Henry with him the next day after work to help him expel Evans. Benjamin warned Evans about the plan. According to the *Herald*, Benjamin's version of the events follows:

> Joshua knocked at the door, and on being asked "who's there?" made no reply, but came in followed by Wilbur and Dimond…he then declared to Dimond that he was in his own house and bid him shut the door. Evans then ordered them out twice, and on Joshua approaching Evans, the latter seized his axe and struck him first with the handle and then with the head. He then felled Dimond and attacked Wilbur, who escaped with a cut in his shoulder.

You can imagine the public outrage such a sensational double homicide would cause. Evans was taken into custody and tried on June 23, 1828. The jurors were all well aware of the man's famous temper and found it easy to believe that he had killed in a fit of rage—even though his attorney insisted that the cornered, threatened man had acted in self defense. Already overwhelmingly biased due to the inescapable publicity the case generated before the trial, the jury returned a verdict of guilty after a mere half hour of deliberations. Evans was sentenced to be hanged on August 22, 1828.

"An immense crowd witnessed the execution, estimated at from fifteen to twenty thousand, many of the spectators coming from fifty miles away," it was reported in the *Herald*. The gallows were "erected on the north bank of the river nearly opposite Hope Chapel," near the current site of the Hope Presbyterian Church on the corner of LeRay and West Main in Watertown. Evans' incarceration had weakened the man, leaving him pale and faint as he took his final steps before the throng of people gathered to see him, and he nearly collapsed as he stood on the gallows waiting for the noose to be readied. "After the drop fell," according to the *Herald*, he struggled for ten minutes before the sheriff cut his lifeless body down. It was taken to the Brownville Cemetery, where a grave had already been dug for the burial, but public outrage resulted in a change of plans before the body could even be lowered into its grave. Instead, it was moved to the edge of town and buried there, somewhere along County Route 54, where it wouldn't upset anyone…or so they thought. But then the vampire sightings began. The superstitious villagers truly believed that Evans had awakened from the dead, seeking vengeance upon all who watched while the hood of death was drawn over his head and the noose secured around his neck. According to several sources, it was agreed that the body would be banished altogether from town, for once and for all. A few of Evans' friends were given the grim task of digging up the corpse after dark, carrying it three or four miles out of town "in the night," and burying it in an unmarked grave at an unknown location—a fact I find hard to believe, since everyone knows you don't disturb a suspected vampire in the night, of all times!

The stigmatized property where the murder occurred is now branded as "Slaughter Hill." The mountain summit, 367 feet above sea level, lies within a triangle formed by three roads between Brownville and Perch River. Even though an apparition (presumably of Evans) was seen in Brownville at the site of the first of the three graves that were dug for him, the other locations mentioned in this story could also be haunted: Slaughter Hill, where Evans' victims died; the location of the former gallows at the corner of LeRay and West Main in Watertown, where Evans (and others) were hanged; the second grave, somewhere out there along a lonely stretch of County Route 54; or that unknown final resting place.

If you happen to venture out that way, beware of a pale man walking toward Slaughter Hill with dark circles under his lifeless, bulging eyes, slight traces of blood drizzling out of the corners of his mouth, and wounds of an indeterminate nature to his neck. Some have said it looks like a vampire. I would counter that it sounds like the sorry specter of a hanged man.

Bibliography

Books

Chester, Alden. *Legal and Judicial History of New York—Volume III*. New York: National Americana Society, 1911.

Curtis, Gates, ed. *History of St. Lawrence County, New York: Our County and its People*. Salem, MA: Higgison Book Co., 1894 (reprint).

Eddy, Daniel. *The Angels' Whispers; Echoes of Spirit Voices*. Boston: Estes and Lauriat, 1881.

Everts, H.L. and J.M. Holcomb. *History of St. Lawrence County, New York*. Syracuse, NY: D. Mason & Company, 1878.

Fowler, Barney. *Adirondack Album*. Schenectady, NY: Outdoor Associates, 1982 (reprint).

-----*Adirondack Album—Volume Two*. Schenectady, NY: Outdoor Associates, 1974.

Frank, Joseph. *Sacred Sites: A Guidebook to Sacred Centers and Mysterious Places*. Woodbury, MN: Llewellyn Publications, 1992.

Hopkins, J. Castell. *French Canada and the St. Lawrence*. Philadelphia: The John C. Winston Co., 1913.

Hough, Franklin B. *A History of Jefferson County in the State of New York*. Watertown, NY: Sterling & Riddell, 1854.

Revai, Cheri. *Haunted Northern New York*. Utica, NY: North Country Books, Inc., 2002.

-----*More Haunted Northern New York*. Utica, NY: North Country Books, Inc., 2003.

-----*Still More Haunted Northern New York*. Utica, NY: North Country Books, Inc., 2004.

-----*Haunted New York: Ghosts & Strange Phenomena of the Empire State*. Mechanicsburg, PA: Stackpole Books, Inc., 2005.

-----*The Big Book of New York Ghost Stories*. Mechanicsburg, PA: Stackpole Books, Inc., 2009.

Seaver, Frederick J. *Historical Sketches of Franklin County and Its Several Towns, With Many Short Biographies*. Albany: JB Lyon Company, 1918.

Web Sites

"1864 Evans Mills." *Roots Web*. Retrieved 22 January 2009. www.rootsweb.ancestry.cm/~nyjeffer/1864evmi.htm

Allen, Ashley Brown. "Hilton Lake Placid Resort." *Hotel F&B*. Retrieved 27 December 2008.

www.hotelfandb.com/boil/march-april2008-hilton-lake-placid.asp

Anne. "The Slightly Haunted LeRay Mansion at Fort Drum." Retrieved 1 February 2009.
http://home.jps.net/~chthonic/Ringwood/other.html

"Anthony Wayne." *Wikipedia*. Retrieved 30 January 2009.
http://en.wikipedia.org/wiki/General_Anthony_Wayne

"Battle of Sackett's Harbor." *Wikipedia*. Retrieved 16 January 2009.
http://en.wikipedia.org/wiki/Battle_of_Sackett%27s_Harbor

"Brief History of Fort Ticonderoga." *Fort Ticonderoga*. Retrieved 9 March 2005.
www.fort-ticonderoga.org/history/brief_history.htm

"Brookside." *Roots Web*. Retrieved 23 January 2009.
www.rootsweb.ancestry.com/~nyjeffer/brkf.htm

"Burke." *Wikipedia*. Retrieved 5 January 2009.
http://en.wikipedia.org/wiki/Burke_(town),_New_York

"Businesses in Evans Mills 1867-1868." *Roots Web*. Retrieved 22 January 2009.
www.rootsweb.ancestry.com

Cady, A. "St. Lawrence County NY Census Files: 1870, 1900, 1920." Retrieved various dates.
http://freepages.genealogy.rootsweb.ancestry.com/~stlawgen/index.HTM

"Campus Map." *St. Lawrence University*: Campus Map. Retrieved 13 January 2009.
www.stlawu.edu/campusmap/map.html

"Dannemora Community United Methodist Church." *Manta*. Retrieved 2 January 2009.
www.manta.com/coms2/dnbcompany_78ztt1

"Decomposition: What is Grave Wax?" *Death Online*. Retrieved 28 January 2009.
www.deathonline.net/decomposition/body_changes/grave_wax.htm

"Definition of Vampire." *Dictionary.net*. Retrieved 24 January 2009. www.dictionary.net/vampire

"Drake Mountain." *New York Places*. Retrieved 1 December 2008.
www.eachtown.com/place.php/id/948631

Drinking Dano. "What is Adipocere?" *Answer Bag*. Retrieved 28 January 2009.
www.answerbag.com/q_view/14859

"Duncan Campbell." *Answers*. Retrieved 30 January 2009.
www.answers.com/topic/Duncan-campbell-british-army-officer

Emerson, Edgar C. "History of Houndsfield (part 3—Sackets Harbor). *History of Houndsfield, NY*. Retrieved 14 January 2009. http://history.rays-place.com/ny/jeff-houndsfield3.htm

"Emily Dickinson (1830-86). Complete Poems. 1924." *Bartleby*. Retrieved 28 January 2009.
www.bartleby.com/113/1092.html

"Facilities—SUNY Potsdam." *SUNY Potsdam*. Retrieved 16 January 2009.
http://www.potsdam.edu/about/facilities.cfm

"Florence (Lee) Whitman." *Cambridge Women's Heritage Project database, W*. Retrieved 13 November 2008. www.cambridgema.gov/cwhp/bios_w.html

"Folklore & Frost." *WPBS-TV*. Retrieved 26 January 2009.
www.wpbstv.org/FolkloreFrost/PhotosTour08.htm

"Fort Leavenworth." *Wikipedia*. Retrieved 2 February 2009.
http://en.wikipedia.org/wiki/Fort_Leavenworth

"Fort Ticonderoga." *Answers*. Retrieved 21 April 2008.
www.answers.com/%22FORT%20TICONDEROGA%22

"Foster." *Our Illustrius Ancestors*. Retrieved 23 January 2009.
http://katharinesweb.net/Ancestors/Ely/Foster.htm

"George I. Mott." *Wikipedia*. Retrieved 5 January 2009.
  http://en.wikipedia.org/wiki/George_I._Mott

"Ghost Stories!" *Project Reality Forums*. Retrieved 29 December 2008.
  www.realitymod.com/forum/f11-off-topic-discussion/13959-ghost-stories.html

"Ghost Stories." *St. Lawrence University*: Sesquicentennial. Retrieved 13 November 2008.
  www.stlawu.edu/150/ghosts.htm

"Ghost Story of Old Stands Up to Tests of Time." *Press-Republican Online*. Retrieved 17 July
  2006. http://archive.pressrepublican.com/Archive/2001/08_2001/08122001gl.htm

"Hail to the Chiefs: A Brief Look at Many of SLU's Leaders." *St. Lawrence University:
  Sesquicentennial*. Retrieved 15 January 2009. www.stlawu.edu/150/presidents.htm

"Haunt in House on Flagg Street." *Strange USA*. Retrieved 2 January 2009.
  www.strangeusa.com/viewLocation.aspx?locationid=6775

"Haunt in Thompson Park." *Strange USA*. Retrieved 29 December 2008.
  www.strangeusa.com/ViewLocation.aspx?locationid=7057

 "Haunted Firehouses (Archive)." *Haunted Firehouses*. Retrieved 22 January 2009.
  http://forums.firehouse.com/archive/index.php/t-15304.html

"Henry Evans." *JeffCoWiki*. Retrieved 21 January 2009.
  http://jeffco.wikispace.com/Henry+Evans

"History of Parishville, NY from *Our County and Its People* by Gates Curtis." History at Rays
  Place. Retrieved 19 November 2008. http://history.rays-place.com/ny/parishville-ny.htm

Home Page. *Evans Mills Volunteer Ambulance Squad*. Retrieved 22 January 2009.
  www.emvas.tripod.com/

Home Page. *Jefferson County Historical Society*. Retrieved 28 October 2008.
  www.jeffersoncounty.history.org/

"Hungerford-L Archives." *Roots Web*. Retrieved 23 January 2009.
  http://archiver.rootsweb.ancestry.colm/th/read/HUNGERFORD/1998-02/0888500655

"Inveraray Ghost Story." *Tales & Stories of Clan Campbell*. Retrieved 4 February 2009.
  http://home.comcast.net/~ccsreg1/tales.htm

"Iroquois Dam." *Table of Contents*. Retrieved 22 August 2008. http://www.stl.nypa.gov/Land%20
  Management%20Plan/St.%20Lawrence%20LMP%20final.102604.htm

"Jabez Foster (1777-1847). *JeffCoWiki*. Retrieved 23 January 2009.
  http://jeffco.wikispaces.com/Jabez+Foster

"James Donatien LeRay (de Chaumont). *JeffCoWiki*. Retrieved 1 February 2009.
  http://jeffco.wikispaces.com/James+D+Leray

"John Brown (abolitionist)." *Wikipedia*. Retrieved 4 January 2009.
  http://en.wikipedia.org/wiki/John_Brown_ (abolitionist)

Katie P. "The Haunted Fort." *Halloween Alliance*. Retrieved 16 January 2009.
  http://halloweenalliance.com/Halloween/the-haunted-fort.htm

Loveland, Dr. Bara H. "Fort Ticonderoga, Upstate NY." *Bio Chakra Research Institute*. Retrieved
  27 January 2009. http://biochakra.com/archives/feb_07.htm

"Loveland Paddock." *JeffCoWiki*. Retrieved 23 January 2009.
  http://jeffco.wikispaces.com/Loveland+Paddock

"Mary Reeser." *Wikipedia*. Retrieved 5 January 2009. http://en.wikipedia.org/wiki/Mary_Reeser

"Methodist Cemetery—Dannemora." *Roots Web*. Retrieved 2 January 2009. http://freepages.
  genealogy.rootsweb.ancestry.com/~frgen/Clinton/Saranac/Dannemora_methodist...

"Moriah, New York." *Wikipedia*. Retrieved 12 December 2008.

http://en.wikipedia.org/wiki/Moriah,_New_York

"North Country's Finest: Halloween Special." *7 News—WWNY-TV* online video archive. Retrieved 16 January 2009. www.wwnytv.net/index.php/2008/10/

"Northern New York Historical Newspapers." *Northern New York Library Network*. http://news.nnyln.org/

Nutt, Amy Ellis. "Mabel Smith's Vision Now Douglass Residential College," (blog) *New Jersey Online*. Retrieved 25 July 2006. www.nj.com/weblogs/print.ssf?/mtlogs/njo_writers/archives/print120293.html

"Nye Manor, Fort Covington, NY—Post-Investigative Report." *NNYPRS*. Retrieved 7 February 2009. www.nnyprs.com/nye_manor.htm

"(Old) Essex County Courthouse." *Flickr*. Retrieved 4 January 2009. http://flickr.com/photos/auvet/2596132720/in/set-72157601286826042/

"Our History—SUNY Potsdam." *SUNY Potsdam*. Retrieved 16 January 2009. http://www.potsdam.edu/about/history.cfm

"Paddock Mansion." *JeffCoWiki*. Retrieved 23 January 2009. http://jeffco.wikispaces.com/Paddock+Mansion

"Parishville, New York." *Wikipedia*. Retrieved 19 November 2008. http://en.wikipedia.org/wiki/Parishville,_New_York

"Perch River Road, Brownville, NY." *Google Maps*. Retrieved 24 January 2009. http://maps.google.com

"Phi Kappa Sigma Fraternity." *St. Lawrence University*. Retrieved 13 November 2008. www.stlawu.edu/map/phikappasigma.html

"President." *St. Lawrence University*. Retrieved 13 November 2008. www.stlawu.edu/president/phikappasigma.html

"Presidential Search." *St. Lawrence University*. Retrieved 13 November 2008. www.stlawu.edu/search09/bios.html

Roizen, Ron. "A Brief History of Clinton Prison." *Corrections History*. Retrieved 3 December 2008. www.correctionhistory.org/northcountry/dannemora/html/clintonhistory3.htm

Rupple, Lisa. "Ghost on the Water." *Zero Time*. Retrieved 7 March 2005. www.zerotime.com/articles/water.htm

"Sackets Harbor Battlefield Alliance." *Sackets Harbor Battlefield*. Retrieved 28 October 2008. www.sacketsharborbattlefield.org/

"Sackets Harbor Battlefield." *1000 Islands*. Retrieved 28 October 2008. www.1000islands.com/sacketsharbor/sackets_harbor_battlefield/

"She-Bear." *Time Magazine* online. Published 16 June 1930. Retrieved 29 December 2008. www.time.com/time/magazine/article/0,9171,739580,00.html

"Slaughter Hill Summit." *Mountain Zone*. Retrieved 24 January 2009. www.mountainzone.com/mountains/detail.asp?fid=7620056

"Stories and Legends," *Ausable Chasm—Chasm*. Retrieved 17 July 2006. http://ausablechasm.com/stories.htm

"SUNY Potsdam: Theatre and Dance." *SUNY Potsdam*. Retrieved 16 January 2009. http://directory.potsdam.edu/?function=dept=Theatre%20and%20Dance

"The BrightSide on Raquette." *BrightSide on Raquette*. Retrieved 11 August 2006. www.brightsideonraquette.com

"The History of Dannemora, N.Y." *Bigelow Society*. Retrieved 2 January 2009. http://bigelowsociety.com/slic/dann1.htm

"The Paddock Mansion." *Jefferson County History*. Retrieved 28 October 2008.
www.jeffersoncountyhistory.org/

"Thompson Park." *Unsolved Mysteries*. Retrieved 29 December 2008.
www.unsolvedmysteries.com/usm280409.html

"Town of Parishville from Child's Gazeteer of St. Lawrence County 1873-74." *Roots Web*.
Retrieved 18 November 2008.
http://freepages.genealogy.rootsweb.ancestry.com/~stlawgen/CHILDS/Parishville.HTM

Untitled image—War of 1812. *Site Mason*. Retrieved 25 January 2009.
www.sitemason.com/files/cs350Q/battleofNO.jpg

Vampire. Dictionary.com. *Webster's Revised Unabridged Dictionary*. MICRA, Inc. Retrieved 21
February 2009. http://dictionary.reference.com/browse/vampire

"Watertown Area Attractions." *What-Where*. Retrieved 28 October 2008.
www.what-where.info/usny_watertown.htm

"Welcome Center (Holcroft House)." *Clarkson*. Retrieved 13 January 2009. http://people.
clarkson.edu/projects/physplantwiki/index.php/Welcome_Center_%28Holcroft_House%29

Newspapers

"A Haunted House." *Massena Observer*. 13 September 1906.

"Accident or Crime—Which?" *Malone Farmer*. 29 August 1906.

Brauchle, Robert. "It has an Appeal to Everyone." *Watertown Daily Times*. 27 December 2008.

"Bullard Given Highest Award." *The Massena Observer*. 16 August 1928.

Bullivant, Todd. "The Haunting of Holcroft." *Clarkson Integrator*. 25 October 1999.

"Canoe Overturns, Two Lake Placid Men Drown." *Adirondack Record-Elizabethtown Post*. 1
November 1923.

"Canton Editor Recalls History of Lee Family." *Massena Observer*. 6 December 1948.

Chapman, Marguerite Gurley. "First Library Association Formed 1814; First Town Hall Built in
1845." *Courier & Freeman*. 29 March 1956.

"Clarkson Urban Legends." *Clarkson Integrator—Freshman Survival Guide*. 25 August 2006.

Condon, Helen. "The Picketville Ghost: A Tale Retold." *Courier & Freeman*. 2 June 1987.

Crawford, Lyle. "Frogman Joins in the Search for Youth Missing Since Kendrew Bridge Fatality.
2,000 People Gather to Watch Operations." *Ogdensburg Advance-News*. 9 December 1951.

"Death List of a Day—John Stebbins Lee." *New York Times*. 20 September 1902.

"Deaths—Mrs. Delisca Desjardins." *The Massena Observer*. 17 April 1973.

"Died While Going Home." *Plattsburgh Sentinel*. 29 March 1889.

"Divers Recover Body from Lake Placid." *Lake Placid News*. 19 September 1963.

"Dr. O. Ward Satterlee Dies at SUCP Office." *Courier & Freeman*. 9 April 1970.

Earl, George. "Alternatives to demolishing old Essex Co. Jail being considered." *Lake Placid
News* (online). 8 May 2008.

"Edwin L. Paddock." *Watertown Herald*. 24 July 1909.

"Fine Old Name Fading Fast—Romantic Story of Clarkson Family." *Commercial Advertiser*. 22
January 1918.

Flynn, Andy. "Last Month was anniversary of Lady in the Lake discovery." *Lake Placid News*. 18 October 1996.

"G.W. Jewett: The Pinnacle." *Watertown Herald*. 24 July 1886.

"Ghost Hunters to Speak at St. Lawrence." *Massena Observer*. 4 January 1979.

"Gift From Annie Clarkson." *St. Lawrence Herald*. 10 June 1927.

"Hanging of Evans." *Watertown Herald*. 16 May 1908.

Harding, Chris. "Clarksons, Friends Once Owned All but 20 Miles of Potsdam Town." *Courier & Freeman*. 8 May 1969.

Harrington, John Walker. "Fort Ticonderoga's International Ghost Story." *New York Times*. 2 July 1922.

"History of Clarkson Family." *Clarkson Integrator*. 10 October 1929.

Hungerford, Edward. "Historic Old Houses of Our Own North Country." *Watertown Daily Times*. Reprinted from 1924 *Country Life in America* series.

"In Memory of Little Hattie." *Plattsburgh Sentinel*. 20 February 1884.

"J. Parkhurst Played Important Part in Fort's Early History." *Fort Covington Sun*. 15 February 1962.

"Lees Ever Loyal to St. Lawrence." *Commercial Advertiser*. 25 April 1922.

"Legends of the St. Lawrence—The Witch of the St. Lawrence." *Massena Observer*. 8 July 1926.

"Local Mention." *Massena Observer*. 25 April 1907.

"Looks Like a Murder." *Chateaugay Record*. 24 August 1906.

Manchester, Lee. "Iron Center Museum." *Lake Placid News*. 24 October 2003.

McKinstry, Lohr. "Covering County Government in Essex County." *Press Republican* (online). 19 March 2007.

McKinstry, Lohr. "Spectrum: Adirondack Haunts." *Press Republican*. 28 October 2007.

"Missing Boy Found Drowned." *Ogdensburg Advance-News*. 6 April 1952.

"Mrs. John Stebbins Lee." *Gouverneur Free Press*. 11 February 1903.

"Mrs. M. O'Neill Passes Away; Rites Thursday." *Massena Observer*. 24 December 1940.

"Mystery at Burke." *Massena Observer*. 30 August 1906.

"News of This County—And the Next." *Lake Placid News*. 13 March 1931.

"North Country Still Talks of Strange Disappearance of Elderly Burke Woman." *Chateaugay Record*. 5 May 1960.

Note re. Emma Wheeler. *Watertown Herald*. 31 October 1896.

"Obituaries—Death of John Parkhurst." *Plattsburgh Sentinel*. 25 August 1882.

"Obituary—John E. Cline." *Massena Observer*. 14 March 1918.

"Obituary—The Late Mrs. Denneen." *The Sun*. 14 July 1921.

"Obituary—William O'Neill." *Massena Observer*. 1 July 1926.

"Old Cemetery in Hopkinton Village." *Courier & Freeman*. 27 October 1909.

Power, Alison. "Ghost Hunters At SLU Raise Friendly Spirit." *Massena Observer*. 16 January 1979.

Reynolds, Kelly L. "Tour Groups in Search of Paranormal Activity." *Watertown Daily Times*. 14 October 2008.

Ross, John A. Jr. "The Founders of Clarkson." *The Integrator*. May 1927.

Rydzewski, John. "Ghost of Holcroft Remains a Mystery." *Clarkson Integrator*. 16 November 1987.

"S.A.E. Home Moves—Family Within." *Commercial Advertiser*. 14 October 1924.

"Shocking Affair at Port Henry." *Plattsburgh Sentinel*. 17 August 1883.

"Still Searching for Body of Pat Greeley." *Lake Placid News*. 2 November 1923.

"Stole Satchel Last March." *Massena Observer*. 4 May 1899.

"T. Streatfield Clarkson." *Norwood News*. 23 September 1902.

"Terrible Story of Mystery and Adventure is Related." *Essex County Republican*. 23 July 1915.

"The Mystery Deepens." *The Adirondack News*. 1 September 1906.

"Traditional bypassed as SUCP buildings given new names." *Courier & Freeman*. 30 May 1973.

"Two Club Employees Drown in Placid Lake." *Lake Placid News*. 26 October 1923.

"University Buys the Old Lee House." *Commercial Advertiser*. 6 March 1928.

Untitled note re. Mary Desmond. *The Palladium*. 26 August 1906.

Untitled note re. P.F. Kezar's boarding house. *Massena Observer*. 2 March 1899.

Untitled note re. Picketville. *Ogdensburg Advance*. 27 August 1891.

Untitled note re. Thomas Supple—Immigration Officer. *Massena Observer*. 9 April 1925.

Untitled notes re. Evans murder case. *Watertown Herald*. 10 November 1900.

Untitled notes re. Holcroft. *Potsdam Herald Record*. 10 December 1926.

Untitled notes re. Thompson Park. *Watertown Herald*. 22 September 1900.

Untitled notes re. Thompson Park. *Watertown Herald*. 24 May 1902.

"Walter Kennedy." *Plattsburgh Sentinel*. 13 May 1930.

Other

Abel, Timothy. "Legends of Public Square Walking Tour Script." Obtained 21 January 2009.

"Personnel & Administration Committee (Minutes)—Monday, May 19, 2008." Essex County Board of Supervisors. Also available online. Obtained 12 December 2008. www.co.essex.ny.us/BdOfSupervisors/.

"Department of Theatre and Dance Handbook 2008-2009." Obtained 16 January 2009.

"*The Hub*—Constitution." Obtained 13 November 2008.

"Haunted Fort Returns to Fort Ticonderoga." Press release from Fort Ticonderoga. Released on 22 September 2008.

Spicer, Marc. Computer-generated diagram of haunted happenings in his home.

About the Author

Cheri Farnsworth has written the following titles, some under the name of Cheri Revai:

Haunted Northern New York (2002)

More Haunted Northern New York (2003)

Still More Haunted Northern New York (2004)

Haunted Massachusetts: Ghosts & Strange Phenomena of the Bay State (2005)

Haunted New York: Ghosts & Strange Phenomena of the Empire State (2005)

Haunted Connecticut: Ghosts & Strange Phenomena of the Constitution State (2006)

Haunted New York City: Ghosts & Strange Phenomena of the Big Apple (2008)

The Big Book of New York Ghost Stories (2009)

Haunted Hudson Valley (2010)

Adirondack Enigma: The Depraved Intellect and Mysterious Life of North Country Wife Killer Henry Debosnys (2010)

Murder & Mayhem in St. Lawrence County (2010)

Alphabet Killer: The True Story of the Double Initial Murders (2010)

Haunted Northern New York Volume 4 (2010)

Author Cheri Farnsworth and "Coco."

Farnsworth is a North Country native who enjoys researching true crime and the link between history and the paranormal. She is a mother of four who works in accounting by day and writes books by night. You may contact the author at PO Box 295, Massena, NY 13662, or email her at farnsworth.cheri@gmail.com. For more information, visit the author's Web site at:

www.cherifarnsworth.com